"What would happen if you fell in love?"

Lucas asked the question harshly. "What if you fell in love with a man who didn't match your father's requirements?"

Lindsay felt a surge of rebellion. "If I loved him and he loved me, then I'd say to hell with my inheritance."

"And you aren't in love with Jeremy."

"You don't know how I feel."

"Like hell I don't!" There was anger in his voice. "I haven't forgotten last night, even if you would prefer to pretend that you have."

"You thought I was your wife..."

"Are you trying to convince me that we were playing make-believe? That you thought I was Jeremy? You knew exactly who I was, and you didn't want me to stop, did you?"

"No!" Lindsay tore herself from his grasp and fled to her room.

Books by Penny Jordan

HARLEQUIN PRESENTS

HARLEQUIN SIGNATURE EDITION

These books may be available at your local bookseller.

Don't miss any of our special offers. Write to us at the following address for information on our newest releases.

Harlequin Reader Service
P.O. Box 52040, Phoenix, AZ 85072-2040
Canadian address: P.O. Box 2800, Postal Station A,
5170 Yonge St., Willowdale, Ont. M2N 6J3

PENNY JORDAN

permission to love

Harlequin Books

TORONTO • NEW YORK • LONDON
AMSTERDAM • PARIS • SYDNEY • HAMBURG
STOCKHOLM • ATHENS • TOKYO • MILAN

Harlequin Presents first edition March 1986
ISBN 0-373-10868-0

Original hardcover edition published in 1985
by Mills & Boon Limited

CHAPTER ONE

'So, it's all settled then. The weekend after next we'll go down to Gloucestershire and break the news to my parents, and of course you'll want to tell your brother.'

'Stepbrother,' Lindsay corrected absently. Since she had accepted Jeremy's proposal, she had had the disconcerting suspicion that he expected her to turn almost overnight from an independent career woman into a dutiful, clinging fiancée, but she quelled all the doubts crowding into her mind, reminding herself that she was twenty-four; old enough and mature enough to accept that it was far better to choose a marriage partner for practical reasons rather than emotional ones. After all Jeremy was everything that her father had wanted for her in a husband. He was something in the City; his parents were comfortably-off landowners and if she personally had not particularly taken to Sir John and Lady Irene then she was not so very much different from thousands of other females who at times found it difficult to get on with their inlaws.

'Brother, stepbrother . . . it's one and the same thing,' Jeremy informed her fussily. 'But you'll have to let him know. The parents will want to hold an engagement party for us and then there'll be the press announcements. It would look rather off if he learned of our engagement second-hand. In fact it might be an idea if we went to see him together this weekend. He'll want to talk to me about handing over the responsibility for your inheritance anyway.'

Something cool flashed in Lindsay's normally warm golden eyes for a moment, but she knew that Jeremy was oblivious to her momentary anger. Jeremy was not a man who felt at ease with female emotions, but it seemed childish to mentally berate him for his lack of understanding of her feelings now, when originally, his calm unflappableness had been one of the things that drew her to him. Ever since she had been seventeen Lindsay had been pursued by the male sex, but she had come to wonder how many of her supposed admirers had wanted her for herself and how many had been drawn to her by the magnet of her father's wealth. She was attractive enough in her own way she supposed, if one liked tall, slender women with slightly irregular features and honey blonde hair, but she would never have described herself as beautiful. Many of her escorts had however. Her full lips thinned slightly. What had they wanted? Her or her inheritance.

Strange to remember that until Lucas's engagement it had never occurred to her to think of herself as a rich prize that a man might marry to secure her wealth.

Her father had over-protected her of course, and perhaps that was natural. The death of her fragile, delicate mother after the birth of her still-born son had had a traumatic effect on her father. For months afterwards he had barely let Lindsay out of his sight. He had blamed himself for her mother's death; she knew that, cursing himself for taking her away from her natural environment and subjecting her to the rigours of life as the wife of a man with his way to make in the world and with no means of doing so other than his own brain and will.

Her parents' marriage had been a true love match. Privately Lindsay thought her mother must have possessed a much stronger personality than her father had thought, otherwise how had she found the courage to leave her parents and everything else that was familiar, behind her, to run away from that luxurious pampered existence to marry the son of her parents' gardener?

At the time the press had been full of the story. When she had been old enough to pick up scraps of gossip Lindsay had gone down to the local library and turned up the old story. Her mother had been eighteen when she ran away with her father. He had been twenty-two and they had been married most romantically at Gretna. In true high emotional fashion Lindsay's grandparents had refused to have anything to do with their erring daughter and it was this unrelenting attitude that had led to her father's determination, obsession almost; that Lindsay should marry into the class that had so cruelly rejected her mother and thereby vindicate her mother's sacrifice in marrying him.

Over the years Lindsay had come to realise that her father's grief had left him scarred and intractable over this issue. Even when he had married for a second time, he had not abandoned his determined stance over Lindsay's marriage. In fact there had been a time when Lindsay suspected that it had been the only thing that kept him alive; his fierce determination that his daughter should

not be looked down upon and rejected as his wife
had been. And he was a wealthy enough man to
ensure that Lindsay should have the best of
everything, including a top-drawer husband. The
financial success which had come too late to save
his delicate wife, was the weapon he was
determined to use against what he considered to be
the rejection of her family. Lindsay had grown up
from the age of seven knowing what her father had
planned for her; knowing and accepting it because
she sensed that to do otherwise would hurt her
father.

Lindsay had grown to care very deeply for her
stepmother. Sheila Armitage had been their
housekeeper, joining the household three years
after her own mother's death. Lindsay had been
ten at the time and had responded readily to
Sheila's warm mothering. She had responded even
more readily to Lucas' affectionate toleration of
her. Seven years her senior, Sheila's son by her
first marriage, Lucas had been Lindsay's god and
when he and her father had struck up a close
rapport, nothing could have pleased her more.
Lucas took the place of the son her father had
always wanted. He was old fashioned in that he
considered all women to be delicate plants to be
shielded from the harsh realities of life, and
because he was her father and she loved him
Lindsay went along with the role he had devised
for her. After leaving school, her father intended
that she was to go to Switzerland to be 'finished'.
His business was expanding rapidly, and Lucas
was his right hand man. Despite the traumas of
being a teenager, Lindsay was conscious of being
happier than she had ever been in her life. Sheila

provided a buffer between her and her father, shielding Lindsay from the full force of his determination. Lindsay had been able to tell Sheila how unsettled she felt; how much she would have preferred to use the brain God had given her and go on to University rather than finishing school, and Sheila had been gently sympathetic.

In fact when she looked back on that last summer before everything had changed so dramatically, she could think of only one jarring note.

It had happened one hot afternoon—a Saturday in July. Over lunch her father had been talking about her future, telling her that he hoped while she was at finishing school she would make the right sort of contacts. He had never made any secret in the family circle of his plans for her, but listening to him Lindsay remembered how she had glanced at Lucas and been shocked by the bitter, grim expression darkening his eyes. It had gone almost the moment she saw it, and later she had wondered what Lucas could have been thinking about. That was before she had known about Gwendolin.

She had gone into the herb garden after lunch, curiously restless and wishing she had the courage to explain to her father that the life he was equipping her for was not necessarily the one she wanted. But she knew how bitterly disappointed he would be ... how hurt ... and she just could not bring herself to deliver the blow. She would tell him later, she comforted herself. Somehow before the summer was over she would find a way ... She had been lying face down, full length on the small camomile lawn when a shadow fell across the sun. Rolling over, she had squinted up into Lucas' shuttered face, her own breaking into a warm smile. Lately whenever she saw Lucas it had become oddly difficult to breathe whenever she was close to her stepbrother. It had occurred to her to wonder if she was suffering from some sort of crush on him, but she had dismissed the idea as ridiculous. Lucas was her brother ... or as good as. As he came down beside her she studied him carefully. Looking at Lucas always gave her a special kind of pleasure. There was something so strong about his features that just to look at them comforted her. Lucas would never allow anyone to push him into a situation he didn't want. He was as dark as she was fair, his hair thick and straight where hers waved. There had been some sort of crisis at the office which had necessitated both him and her father working late, and as a consequence he had not had time to get his hair cut and it curled thickly down over the collar of his shirt.

His face was all planes and angles, hard boned and very male. There were times like now when she wanted to reach out and touch him; to see if the living flesh felt as hard as it looked, but something always stopped her. Lucas had always had a certain remoteness about him; an air which warned against taking too many intimacies. His eyes, searched her face with cool grey precision, almost as though he were looking for something, and Lindsay felt herself tremble.

'I don't want to go to Switzerland.' The words burst from her before she could stop them, a childish plea, which she regretted instantly. She was sixteen, not six, she told herself angrily.

'Then you must tell your father so.' Lucas

sounded cold and remote. He wasn't going to help her, Lindsay could see that.

'He won't listen to me ... I don't want to hurt him.'

She could feel thick tears blurring her throat, closing it up and she hung her head in anguish.

'And because of that you'll sacrifice yourself to marriage with some idiotic county type who'll marry you for your father's money. Is that really what you want from life Lindsay?'

It was so unlike him to be so cruel to her that Lindsay could say nothing. Tears flowed hotly down her face, but she made no move to check them, or to hide them from him. She heard the thick exclamation he made in his throat and through her own pain was dimly aware of something in his eyes that could have been pity and then she was in his arms, being comforted and rocked as she had been on countless occasions in the past. Much as he loved her, her father was not a demonstrative person, and it was always to Lucas that she turned for warmth and physical affection.

'I'm sorry, I shouldn't have spoken to you like that.' His fingers, rough and slightly calloused brushed away her tears, 'But Lindsay, can't you see what's going to happen to you if you don't take charge of your own life. Can't you see what you'll be missing if you go along with your father's plans for you?'

She had managed a watery smile and asked mistily, 'Like what?'

'Like this.'

The sensation of having Lucas' mouth moving against her own almost robbed her of the ability to breathe. She was dimly conscious of her heart racing madly, thudding against her chest wall. Her lips softened beneath the cool assault of Lucas's and then abruptly he was pushing her away and standing up, his expression morose and brooding as he looked down at her.

'If you settle for the life your father's planning for you that's what you'll be missing Lindsay ... reality and all the pleasures and pains that go with it.'

He was gone before she could speak, and she remembered she had touched her mouth wonderingly. Lucas had kissed her many times before but never like that. A little shiver ran down her spine, and she was conscious of a sudden restlessness, an excess of energy that demanded some outlet.

It seemed hard to believe that the man who had spoken to her like that was the same one who eighteen months later was urging her to accept the proposal of the son of a neighbouring landowner; a young man who fulfilled all the qualifications her father wanted for her in a husband and yet who sexually left her completely cold. Tears stung her eyes and Lindsay was surprised to find them there. She was aware that Jeremy had gone quiet and raised her eyes to meet his.

'Where were you?' he questioned coolly. 'You know Lindsay you'll have to stop going off into daydreams like that, otherwise my family's going to think you're not quite right in the head.'

'But since I'm an extremely wealthy heiress, they'll be prepared to overlook it?' She said the words with a smile, but knew she had shocked Jeremy from his expression. 'You know you're beginning to get quite a hang-up about this money,' he told her curtly.

'Would you want to marry me if I didn't have it?'

Be honest with me Jeremy she prayed inwardly, I'm so sick of sycophantic men whispering words of love when what they love is not me but my bank balance ... And yet she wanted to be married ... to have children, a home, roots ... perhaps because of the loss of her mother when she was so young and then the double blow of her father and stepmother's deaths in a plane crash that summer she was seventeen. Those losses had left her with a deep-seated need for security perhaps, but not at any price.

She saw Jeremy's slightly uncomfortable expression, but he responsed with dogged honestly. 'I don't know ... All my life I've been brought up with the responsibility that the family needs money,' he told her half curtly. 'That's just the way it is. I'm thirty years old Lindsay and you're twenty-four ... can't you accept that we're both the type of people whose passions don't run very deep. That doesn't mean to say that because...'

'Sexually we don't turn one another on?' Lindsay supplied wryly for him, watching the angry colour creep up under his skin.

'I thought we'd agreed we'd wait until we were married,' Jeremy interposed stiffly. 'After all ... we're not teenagers ... you share your flat and I share mine, and ...'

Suddenly Lindsay was tired of tormenting him. Was it his fault that like her he had been brought up to accept that his future lay along certain lines? She knew all about Jeremy's family. Her flat mate

Caroline was a distant cousin of his. The title went back to Regency times and since the first world war the family had had to struggle to hold on to their land. Jeremy's grandmother had been the daughter of a wealthy American, but Jeremy's father had been one of four children and their mother had insisted that her money was divided equally between them. Jeremy himself had two younger sisters. As the only son it was his duty to marry someone wealthy enough to help him retain the family home. Lindsay could understand Jeremy's position. She also suspected that his family were not too keen on her. She had met them all at Christmas. His mother had been coolly distant; his father over-jovial. Lindsay had sensed them thinking that she was not really their type; she loathed hunting for instance and Jeremy's father was Master of the local Hunt. She also had a career whilst Jeremy's mother had made it clear that anyone who married her son would have to devote herself to the type of committee/good works life she enjoyed. She was torn, Lindsay knew that. She and Jeremy had known each other for several years. She had met him through Caroline and they had several interests in common. She knew he would make her a good husband—if somewhat dull. He was a very placid man, stuffy in some ways perhaps as befitted a junior partner in an old established firm of stockbrokers. He tended to look down on Lindsay's work. She worked for one of the foremost Unit Trust organisations in the country, and the salary she earned through selling their Unit Trusts was phenomenal. There was more of her father in her than he had ever suspected, she often thought. She enjoyed the cut and thrust of her business life, and yet another side of her, her mother's side perhaps, yearned for a home and children.

'Sex isn't everything.' Jeremy looked embarrassed as he made the comment. Lindsay had discovered early on in their relationship that anything to do with such a personal topic embarrassed him. When she had first guessed that he intended to propose to her she had suggested they went away on holiday together. She was a virgin by choice, never having met any man whose touch or kisses aroused her to the point where she craved his possession and she desperately wanted to feel at least some of that craving for Jeremy, but he had been horrified by her suggestion. Rather stiffly he had told her that he had too much respect for her to take advantage of her suggestion; indeed he had gone on to say that he had heard that she had a reputation for being unobtainable sexually and she had sensed then that this had pleased him. She had chosen Jeremy freely and yet every now and then nagging doubts arose. Was there perhaps something wrong with her? Was she totally incapable of intense sexual desire? There were people with low libidoes and if she was one of them it was as well that she was marrying a man like Jeremy.

Contrite, she proferred a brief smile. 'No, perhaps you're right,' she agreed.

Relieved Jeremy smiled back at her. 'So you'll arrange for us to visit your brother and his wife this weekend?'

Sensing his impatience to return to his office, Lindsay nodded her head. She wasn't looking

forward to going down to Dorset but it would
have to be done. Although she was well over age
for a legal guardian, she still had to have Lucas'
approval to her prospective husband before she
could come into her inheritance, and Jeremy
would not want her without it. Not that Lucas was
likely to disapprove. Jeremy was everything her
father had wanted for her in a husband. Who
would have thought that Lucas could change so
much? Jeremy was paying the bill; Lindsay stood
up. She intended going straight back to her flat
after lunch. She had taken the afternoon off, but
there was some paperwork she wanted to catch up
on. Jeremy kissed her briefly on the cheek before
depositing her in a taxi. His lips were dry and and
faintly chill. Sighing, Lindsay gave the driver her
address.

Lucas had bought the flat for her when she first
came to London and it was situated in an elegant
Regency block. At first she had raged that she
could manage on her own, but a month of living in
grotty digs, feeding herself on beans and toast
every night had soon brought her down to earth. It
had been Lucas who insisted on her advertising
for a flat-mate and who had carefully vetted the
applicants. She had taken little interest in the
proceedings. It had been pride and nothing more
that had led to her leaving home, and the pain of
parting from all that she loved; the pain of being
betrayed by the one person she had thought would
never let her down had anaesthetised her against
feeling anything else.

She had worked hard to get where she was and
she was proud of her success. Jeremy wanted her
to give up work when they married. Sighing

faintly, Lindsay paid off her taxi and walked towards her front door.

She had decorated the flat herself, choosing soft, feminine shades of peaches and greys and she was very pleased with the effect of the pale peachy rag-rolled walls, and the soft, plain grey carpet. Ignoring the large sitting room she went instead into her own small study. Because of the nature of her work her hours were flexible and she could if she chose, work at home in preference to in an office, and her flatmate knew that this particular room was out of bounds to everyone apart from Lindsay herself.

It should have been the easiest thing in the world to simply pick up the 'phone and tell Lucas that she was going down this weekend.

It hadn't come as a surprise to her on her father's death to learn that he had appointed Lucas as her guardian and that he had left Lucas in charge of his business empire. The house had been left to them jointly but there was a stipulation in her father's will that unless she married, Lucas would always have control of her inheritance and that when she did marry it must be to a man whom Lucas approved of.

She had been stunned by this knowledge, but at sixteen the trauma of coping with the death of her father and Sheila had vastly overridden any concern she might have felt about the will.

Her father had been dead for three months before she began to realise how much Lucas had changed. For a start he had tried to insist that she went to finishing school as her father had wanted her to. That had been his first betrayal and the shock of it had caused her almost as much pain as

her father's death. Lucas himself had been the one
to tell her to make her own way in life, but when
she tackled him about this he had simply said
grimly that things had changed.

It was about that time that she had first become
aware of Gwendolin. She had never particularly
liked the older girl, who was the daughter of her
father's solicitor, and her constant visits to the
house under the guise of 'helping' made her feel
extremely prickly. She wasn't a child, she
remembered telling Lucas hotly on one occasion;
she was more than capable of seeing that they ate
proper meals ... and that the house was kept
clean.

After Sheila had married her father they had
never taken on another housekeeper, Sheila
preferred to manage with help from the village,
and at the time she had not properly understood
Lucas' grim, 'That you're not!'

Which only went to prove how much of a child
she actually had been. No. It had taken
Gwendolin to open her eyes to the truth. People
were talking about her and Lucas, she had told
Lindsay spitefully. And when she had asked why,
Gwendolin had pointed out that they weren't
related by blood. 'I've seen the way you look at
him,' she had added nastily. 'Poor Lucas, he must
find it difficult to deal with such a mammoth
crush. It isn't fair to him at all of your father to
have landed him with the responsibility of you.
And what about when he marries?'

Lucas married? A coldness had crept through
her limbs. 'What's the matter,' Gwendolin had
demanded acidly. 'Surely you realise that Lucas is
an extremely virile man? Naturally he will marry

... and when he does you can hardly suppose his wife will want a teenage stepsister on her hands.'

Lindsay knew without having to hear it in so many words that when Gwendolin talked of Lucas' wife, it was herself she had in mind. A deep pain tore through Lindsay when she turned the conversation over in her mind later. She didn't want to lose Lucas as well ... not so soon after losing her father and Sheila, and marriage would take him away from her ... she knew that.

Gwendolin hadn't been content to leave matters there. She had told Lindsay in Lucas' hearing that people were starting to talk ... that there were those who thought it wrong for a teenage girl to live so closely with a man who after all was no blood relation to her. Lindsay had been instantly defensive. 'Lucas might not be my brother,' she had cried painfully, 'but I love him as one ...' Can't you see, she had wanted to say, he's all I've got left, but the words had stuck in her throat, and later on when Lucas had changed from the warm, smiling man she knew into a grim-faced stranger she had been filled with dread.

At first when he had insisted on taking her out with him when he went visiting their neighbours she had thought it was because he wanted her company, but her pleasure had turned to pain when she realised the truth. He was trying to get her married and off his hands.

He gave her the ultimatum the night after Richard Browne had approached him for permission to marry her. Either she accepted Richard or she went to finishing school.

His treatment of her had hurt her bitterly. Where was the Lucas she knew and loved? All her

appeals to him met with stubborn resistance. He
had even flinched away from her when she tried to
touch him, his eyes cold and hard. 'You can't stay
here alone with me,' he had told her bluntly.

It was then that she had grown up. 'Not quite six
months ago you were telling me to take charge of my
own life, Lucas,' she had reminded him coolly.

His smile had been openly derisive. 'That was
before I realised how incapable of doing so you
are. You've been brought up almost from birth to
fulfil one purpose and one alone Lindsay. Your
father has made it plain what he expects me to do
. . . I owe him too much to ignore his wishes.'

'But I don't want to go to finishing school and
I don't want to marry Richard.'

He had looked at her broodingly after her
passionate outburst and then asked, 'So, what do
you want to do.'

What might have happened if she hadn't said
those next foolish words? There was no knowing.
'I want to stay here with you,' she had told him
emotionally.

His whole expression had changed, hardening,
rejecting her silent plea for understanding.

'What as Lindsay?' he had demanded harshly,
'My bed-mate? Because that's what everyone will
think you are. Look at yourself.' He had spun her
round so that she could see her own reflection in
the mirror. 'Although you may not know it yet
there's a potent streak of sensuality in your nature.
You might be innocent, but you don't look it, and
if we continue to live here alone, your reputation
will be ruined.'

There were so many things she could have
said—they could have got a housekeeper . . . they

could have ... but what was the use of thinking
that now. His announcement had shocked her,
stunned her into silence and pain. All she was
aware of was his rejection. Did he, like Gwendolin,
think she harboured some secret love for him. Was
that why he was so keen to get rid of her. Pain
heaped up on pain and suddenly all she wanted to
do was to be free ... free to escape from Lucas
and from her pain.

She had left that night, taking with her a
suitcase and Post Office savings book.

It hadn't taken Lucas long to track her down to
the dingy lodgings which were all she had
managed to afford. One look at his grimly angry
face as he opened the door and stared at her had
killed for all time any childish longing she might
still have had that she could run into the safe
harbour of his arms and that everything would be
made all right.

'Pack your things, I'm taking you home.' That
was all he said to her, and it wasn't until he had
got her back to Dorset that he broke the shattering
news to her that he was going to marry
Gwendolin. Of course she knew that Gwendolin
wanted him. The look in the older woman's eyes
when she looked at him was openly obvious,
embarrassingly so, but although Lucas had had
plenty of girlfriends, Lindsay had never seen him
single Gwendolin out for any special attention, but
now he was telling her he was going to marry her.
Remembering Gwendolin's claim that no wife of
Lucas' would want her around, she announced
grimly that he had wasted his time in bringing her
back because the moment the wedding was over
she was going to leave.

They had argued about it up until the wedding and beyond. Lucas had even postponed having a honeymoon because he did not trust her not to run away while he was gone. After he had married, his temper had become even more savage, and Lindsay had suffered several verbal maulings from him because he eventually conceded that it might be best for her to live away from home. He had suggested university, but by that stage she was in no mood to fall in with any of his suggestions and so had insisted on London. What a trial she must have been to him. It was no wonder he was always so cool and distant to her on the rare occasions when she did go back. Her father had left the house to them jointly . . . but she never thought of it as home now. Gwendolin had brought in a firm of designers once she and Lucas were married, and although the results were very stylish Lindsay found them cold and unappealing. But now she would have to go back. Lucas would have to know she was getting married and Jeremy was right. It would be both silly and childish to leave him to find out second or even third hand. And what was more, it would be cowardly too, Lindsay admitted. She had been avoiding facing Lucas for far too long.

CHAPTER TWO

THE soft Dorset burr of the woman who answered the telephone was unfamiliar to her. Gwendolin had employed a live-in couple from Barbados when she and Lucas were first married, and Lindsay wondered if perhaps they had left. If so, she was not surprised. In her opinion Gwendolin had overworked them unmercifully. But never when Lucas was there. No, Lindsay had learned early on in her relationship with the older woman that Gwendolin presented a far different face to those whom she wanted to impress than she did to those she didn't, and Lindsay herself, and her staff were patently among those she did not.

At first when Lucas had announced that he was to marry Gwendolin she had been shocked, and yes hurt somehow, although she knew the latter emotion to be an unreasonable one. Of course it was natural that Lucas should want to marry. He had had many girlfriends, some of whom she had liked in a luke-warm sort of way and some of whom she had not, but at the time he had made his announcement to her she had been almost overwhelmed by something approaching revulsion that he should even contemplate marrying Gwendolin. For one thing she had pursued him so blatantly that Lindsay had been sure Lucas would reject her on those grounds alone. For another it was widely gossiped locally that Gwen had had more than one affair. She had been no inexperienced girl when she married Lucas, and Lindsay vividly remembered her own sense of inadequacy and embarrassment when Gwendolin had once mocked her for her own inexperience. She shivered slightly even now, not wanting to picture Lucas and Gwen as lovers, but unable to stop herself from doing so, images of Lucas' athletic naked body sensually entwined with that of his dark-haired wife. The sensations aroused by the images stunned her. Distaste caused nausea to rise up in her throat and almost choke her. What was wrong with her that she could feel like this about another couple and yet when it came to Jeremy . . . or any other man for that matter . . . she felt so intrinsically cold?

Gathering her thoughts together she asked to speak to Lucas and was told by the new housekeeper who introduced herself as Mrs James that he was away on business overnight.

'Yes,' she confirmed she did expect him back by the weekend, when Lindsay introduced herself. Forcing down her reluctance Lindsay asked to speak to Gwendolin. There was a small hesitant pause before Mrs James said uncertainly, 'I'm afraid Mrs Armitage is not here either.'

Taking a chance, Lindsay arranged with Mrs James that she and Jeremy would arrive late Friday evening. As they had to go and visit Jeremy's parents the following weekend, she would have to tell Lucas about her forthcoming engagement soon, and although she would have preferred to do so by 'phone, Jeremy who was a stickler for everything that was proper and correct, would frown over her doing so.

It amazed her that after all this time the rift that

had opened up between herself and Lucas that last summer, should still hurt her so much. She was six years older for goodness sake, no longer a teenager but an adult herself. At Gwendolin's insistence she had always spent Christmas at home with them, but she had always found her visits uncomfortable occasions, longing for them to be over. Gwendolin was an extremely social person and the house always seemed to be packed with guests; friends of hers in the main, unknown to Lindsay and whom she did not find particularly convivial. Lucas always remained remote and cold towards her appearing, so it seemed to avoid her company, reminding her shamingly of Gwendolin's assertions that he had found Lindsay's feelings for him embarrassing and annoying. In many ways it did not surprise her that they had not had children— Gwendolin was the most unmaternal woman she had ever met, but Lucas, she remembered had always been good with them and she would have expected him to want a family of his own.

Sighing faintly as she replaced the receiver, she tried to concentrate on her work, but her mind kept wandering, replaying memories from her childhood, Lucas ... playing tennis with her, coaching her ... Lucas, helping her with her homework ... The warmth he had always shown her and the loneliness she had felt when he went to university. She heard a door slam and realised that Caroline was back. Her flatmate poked her head round the study door, having knocked briefly.

'Busy?' she enquired, 'Or do you fancy a coffee?'

'I'd love one. I ought to be working,' Lindsay admitted, 'but I just can't turn my mind to it.'

'Mmm ... I wonder why. Most unlike you.'
Caroline looked at her shrewdly. 'Your inability to
concentrate wouldn't have anything to do with a
certain cousin of mine would it?'

'Sort of. We're going down to see Jeremy's
parents the weekend after next,' Lindsay told her,
answering her unspoken question.

Caroline grimaced faintly and rolled her eyes.
'Poor you. His mother's a bit of a stickler.
Jeremy's the apple of her eye of course, and no girl
could possibly be worthy of him. Of course you
have got one thing in your favour.'

'My money you mean?' Lindsay stood up with
fluid grace, kneading the tension knots at the back
of her neck. 'Mmm ...'

'Still you're hardly springing a surprise on
them,' Caroline comforted. 'Ma was saying the
last time I went home that it was high time the
pair of you got engaged. What about your family?'

'Well there's only Lucas of course,' Lindsay told
her. 'Jeremy and I are going down to see him this
weekend.'

'Lucky you.' Caroline dimpled a smile of
feminine envy at her. 'It's just as well that he's
your stepbrother and safely married, otherwise
poor Jeremy wouldn't stand a chance.' She saw
Lindsay's expression and grinned. 'Oh come on
Lin, surely even you can see that he's living,
breathing temptation to our poor vulnerable sex.
The dreadful thing is that he doesn't even seem to
be aware of the effect he has on us. I wonder what
he ever saw in Gwendolin.'

'She's very attractive,' Lindsay responded
weakly, feeling honour-bound to defend her
stepsister-in-law.

'Sure if you like icebergs,' Caroline came back forthrightly, 'I'm sure she doesn't have an ounce of human warmth in her, and Lucas never strikes me as being a man who's madly in love with his wife, does he you?'

'He's always been adept at hiding his feelings . . .'

'Is that what it is? Sometimes I get the feeling he's put them into cold storage,' Caroline came back. 'I wonder if he's faithful to her?'

She saw her flat-mate's expression and grimaced. 'Okay, so he's everything the perfect husband should be, but she's very far from being the perfect wife. I didn't say anything before but when I was in Gstaad this winter I saw her there . . . and not with Lucas.'

'She's a very keen skier,' Lindsay told her a little stiffly, 'Lucas is a busy man . . . perhaps he couldn't get away. And anyway just because you saw her with another man that doesn't mean . . .'

'That she's having an affair with him? Don't you believe it,' Caroline told her. 'They might have had separate rooms and they might have been discreet but they were lovers all right . . . you can't mistake the signs.'

'Don't tell me . . . I don't want to hear any more,' Lindsay wanted to plead, and like a warning bell, a comment of Lucas' surfaced from the past. 'You always want to avoid awkward situations Lindsay, but you can't spend the rest of your life doing that. One day I hope you're going to opt for pleasing yourself rather than simply pleasing others.'

And it was true. Intelligent; attractive, popular, she knew she was all of those things and yet deep inside herself she saw herself as a coward. As a child she had striven desperately hard after her mother's death to please her father . . . to take the place of the woman they had both lost, and had always been nagged by the feeling that she had somehow failed; that the intelligence and stamina she had inherited from him, detracted, in his eyes, from her character and that he would have preferred her to be more like her delicate, hesitant mother. At school too, she had tried to please, breaking the pattern only that summer she had been sixteen, and then of course with Lucas. Lucas was the only person she suddenly realised, with whom she had been able to be properly herself. He had always encouraged her to state her own opinion, to argue with him if she felt so inclined. Lucas had never demanded that she fitted herself into any preconceived ideas he might have about her. But Lucas had changed when her father died; he had ceased being a beloved brother and mentor and become instead a remote, cold stranger, who no longer hugged or touched her in any way; who did not encourage her to talk to him and who eventually married Gwendolin, thus ensuring that there would be a gulf between them for ever. Was Caroline right? Was Gwen unfaithful to him? But why? She had never made any secret of her desire for Lucas. She had in fact pursued him relentlessly, so why break her marriage vows and take a lover?

'Seeing Jeremy tonight?' Caroline enquired, changing the subject. Lindsay shook her head. 'I need an early night. I'm taking a break from the office next week, so I want to clear my desk first.'

'Are you and Jeremy going away?'

Once again Lindsay shook her head. 'No. I haven't had a break yet this year. I thought I might do a little bit of shopping . . . unwind a bit, relax . . .'

'Mmm . . . well I'd better fly. Simon's taking me to dinner, and if I don't get a move on I won't be ready.'

Simon was the new man in Caroline's life. Her menfriends lasted on average a matter of weeks rather than months, and unlike Lindsay she was constantly falling in and out of love.

Lindsay finished work early on Friday afternoon and returned home to pack. She had almost finished when the 'phone rang. Her nerves tensed totally unexpectedly, and until she picked up the receiver and heard Jeremy's familiar voice she didn't realise that her tension had been in case the caller was Lucas.

'Lindsay I've got some bad news,' Jeremy began without preamble. 'I'm not going to be able to make it this weekend. Something's come up and I have to fly up to Scotland to see a client.'

There had been several occasions recently when Jeremy had had to work at the weekend, and as Lindsay suppressed her annoyance she heard him saying, 'Look why don't you go home as planned—after all, you're going to want to tell your brother about our engagement before we make it public. My parents will want to put a notice in the *Times*, once we've made things official next weekend.'

What Jeremy was saying made good sense, Lindsay knew that and yet she was filled with an intense feeling of reluctance to do as he suggested. She didn't want to see Lucas without the protection of Jeremy's presence, but why?

Shaking aside her nebulous fears, she spoke to Jeremy for several more minutes, eventually agreeing that she would go ahead as they had planned.

Once she had replaced the receiver she wandered into her bedroom wondering what to wear for the journey, and eventually settling on an attractive soft green wool crêpe pleated skirt with a toning sweater. The green reinforced the unusual tawniness of her eyes, and her skin which tanned well, glowed softly golden. They had had a good spring and early summer, and the sun had bleached her hair slightly adding natural highlights, but as she applied her make-up with deft, practised strokes Lindsay was unaware of her own attractions. She didn't want to go home, she recognised unhappily, but she had to ... It's only for one weekend, she reminded herself, and yet inwardly she was dreading it; dreading seeing Lucas ... and of course Gwendolin.

She left London an hour later, driving the Escort car she had bought for herself several months earlier. By most people's standards she and Jeremy could live quite comfortably on their joint salaries, but of course Jeremy had responsibilities towards the estate—heavy and expensive responsibilities, which she suspected were the main reason he was marrying her. What did she want, she asked herself in exasperated impatience as she automatically turned her car in the direction of her home. She didn't love Jeremy passionately herself and yet here she was questioning his own lack of passion for her. Hadn't she accepted yet, in spite of all the evidence to support it, that she was simply not a woman with deeply passionate sexual feelings?

The late afternoon traffic was heavy and she forced herself to switch her attention from her unprofitable thoughts to her driving.

As she drove westward, Lindsay found the traffic gradually thinning out and when she took the familiar turning off the motorway several miles before Bath, she had the narrow road almost all to herself.

Almost all too soon she was driving through the familiar villages, the last one, Hinton St Jude, still as chocolate box pretty as ever with its thatched roofed cottages, their front gardens a rich blaze of colour. It was only a couple of miles from the village to the house, a small square Georgian building set in attractive parklands.

The electrically operated gates stood open and Lindsay's stomach muscles clenched as she drove through. She was dreading the weekend more and more with every moment that passed.

She parked her car in front of the house, a little surprised to find the gravel parking area otherwise empty. Climbing out of the car without pausing to check her make-up or hair she walked up to the front door. It still seemed strange to be knocking on the door of what was legally at least still her home, but Gwendolin had made it quite plain shortly after her marriage that Lessings was now her home, and that as its mistress she expected Lindsay to behave as a guest.

Five minutes went by without any sign of anyone coming to answer her knock. She still had her old keys—it had seemed foolish to keep them but for some reason she had, and feeling more like an intruder than a member of the household, she fished through her bag for the front door keys, wondering as she inserted them into the lock if they would still work or if Gwendolin had had the locks changed. The door swung open easily as the key fitted, and once she was inside the hall, a wave of nostalgia overwhelmed her as she breathed in the unmistakable scents of pot-pourri and wax polish. In her mother's and then Sheila's day the house had always smelled like this, and it had been a smell she loved, but Gwendolin hated it, describing it as medieval, and the bowls of pot-pourri and the old fashioned beeswax had been banished. Now it seemed both were back.

Standing at the foot of the stairs, Lindsay called out experimentally, but there was no response. The distinct feeling that she was alone in the house would not leave her, and she walked slowly into the kitchen. Where was everyone?

A note was propped up conspicuously on the refectory table, and Lindsay picked it up skimming through it. At least she now had an explanation for the housekeeper's absence. It seemed her sister had been involved in a car accident and she had been called in to take care of her. But where was Gwen? Her sister-in-law, Lindsay remembered had an extremely active social life, but even so she felt a tiny prick of annoyance that there was no one here to welcome her. She left the kitchen and wandered back through the hall into the immaculate drawing room. Gwen had called in a team of interior designers shortly after her marriage, and

Lindsay had never liked the cold sophisticated rooms they had created. She had preferred the faded chintzes of her mother's and Sheila's time, and she grimaced in faint distaste at the sterile purity of the now almost all white and chrome room.

As she remembered the only room the designers had not been allowed to touch were the kitchen and Lucas' study, and her old bedroom.

Lucas! Her stomach felt as though it had suddenly been twisted painfully, her nerves so on edge that she felt acute nausea. Where was he? At work no doubt at this time of day. Her mouth hardened slightly. Couldn't he even be bothered to come home to welcome her? *Welcome* her? A harsh bitter laugh escaped her compressed lips and echoed into the thick silence. That would be the day. No doubt he was as anxious to get his weekend over with as she was herself.

And yet, almost without volition her footsteps led her in the direction of his study. The door was half open and Lindsay walked in, a puzzled frown creasing her forehead as she saw the neat pile of correspondence on his desk. She walked closer and saw on the top of one pile a neatly written note in what she now recognised as the housekeeper's handwriting. 'Miss Lindsay 'phoned', it read, 'she and a friend are coming down for the weekend. I have put Miss Lindsay in her old room and her friend in the guest suite.'

Lindsay thought quickly. Did this mean that Lucas didn't *know* she was coming down this weekend? But why would the housekeeper leave a note for Lucas? Why not simply tell Gwen?

Frowning deeply Lindsay made her way back to
the kitchen and filled the kettle. While she was
waiting for it to boil she pondered on what she
ought to do. Plainly whatever business had taken
Lucas away from home had delayed him and the
housekeeper had not had an opportunity to inform
him of her visit. On the other hand it was equally
plain that he was expected home imminently—the
fridge was full of food for one thing. Although it
was tempting to simply get back in her car and
return to London all she would be doing was
putting off the eventual ordeal. She hadn't realised
until now how much she had been nerving herself
for this meeting. If she left without seeing Lucas
she would have it all to live through again. The
kettle boiled and Lindsay automatically went
through the motions of making herself a pot of
tea. She would take it upstairs with her and have a
shower. That might help her to relax. At least she
knew where she was sleeping. If, when Gwen came
back she objected to the way she, Lindsay, had
made herself at home, well she had only herself to
blame for not being on hand to receive her. Her
mind made up Lindsay poured her tea and went
back into the hall.

  Her bedroom had not suffered too much from
the decorators; the theme of lemon and white she
had chosen as a teenager was still retained; the
bedhangings, curtains and chair were all in a soft
lemon and white chintz, the carpet a toning pale
lemon. Lucas had been the one to suggest that she
was old enough for a more grown-up colour
scheme than the old pink and white she had had
since childhood—he had arranged for her room to
be redecorated as a fifteenth birthday surprise, she

remembered. She had been so excited and thrilled
... Sighing faintly she went back downstairs;
garaged her car at the back of the house and
brought up her suitcase.

She had just stepped out of the shower when she
became aware of someone's presence in her
bedroom. Thinking it must be Gwendolin she
pulled on her robe hurriedly, grimacing faintly as
the thin silk clung to her still damp skin, and
opened her shower room door.

It wasn't Gwen who stood there watching her
but Lucas, his dark eyebrows drawn together in a
frown, his skin stretched almost too tightly over
the bones of his face.

'Lindsay ... what the devil ...'

There was a grimness to his mouth that Lindsay
well remembered, but the pain darkening his eyes
was new, and so too was the tiredness plainly
discernible in his drawn features and almost gaunt
frame.

Suddenly becoming aware from the way he was
looking at her, of the flimsiness of her damp robe,
Lindsay hugged her arms protectively around her
body, and muttered crossly. 'I thought you were
Gwendolin ...'

'Now why, I wonder should you think that.'

The tiredness was gone and in its place was a
febrile bitterness that mocked and taunted. 'What
are you doing here?'

His tormenting was replaced by curt anger, and
it lit a corresponding flame of anger in Lindsay.

'This is still my home,' she reminded him, her
chin lifting belligerently, 'even though you have
contrived to make it as uncomfortable a one as
possible for me.'

He had the grace to colour faintly, but there was no remorse in his eyes as they locked on her face. 'I repeat, what are you doing here.'

'Nothing that you need worry about,' Lindsay told him acidly, 'In fact I think when you hear what I've got to say you'll be pleased. I'm getting engaged.'

'Engaged!'

Just for a moment she thought he looked shocked, ill almost but instantly his expression changed to be replaced by one of cynical mockery. 'Well, Well . . . and who is the fortunate man?'

'Jeremy Byles,' Lindsay told him curtly. Why was it that every time they met they rubbed one another raw like this? If they could not regain their old camaraderie, surely they could still meet as civilised human beings; not the snapping snarling enemies the sight of one another seemed to turn them into. 'Jeremy was to have accompanied me here . . . he wanted to advise you of our engagement before his parents make a formal announcement next week.'

A bitter smile curved the thin mouth. 'To advise me of it, or to gain my approval?' Lucas queried. 'He does know the terms of your father's will I take it?'

'Of course.' Bitter anger flashed in Lindsay's topaz eyes, 'but you need not worry Lucas, Jeremy is everything my father would have wanted for me in a husband.'

'Which is why you chose him?'

'Am I allowed to marry for any other reason?' Until she had said it she hadn't realised how much of a burden her father's wishes were to her. She didn't love Jeremy she acknowledged, at least not as she had once dreamed of loving a man, and she could sense the speculation in the look Lucas was giving her.

'Since you can't produce your fiancé for my inspection and approval, I can't see that there was much point in coming down here,' he infuriated her by saying. 'Why did you?'

'I'd already made my plans.' Lindsay was seething ... her temper, normally so slow to ignite already at danger point. 'This is my home, Lucas,' she reminded him sharply, 'I don't need your permission to come here, no matter how unwelcome you choose to make me. Jeremy is everything my father wanted for me in a husband,' she pointed out for a second time. 'You could have no possible grounds for refusing to ...'

'Hand your inheritance over to him? Poor Lindsay, do I really keep you so short of money that you're obliged to marry the first blue-blooded idiot you can find?'

'It has nothing to do with the money—at least not on my side, you must know that,' Lindsay stormed back at him.

'Then why so concerned about my approval? True love needs no approval.' He all but sneered the words at her, and Lindsay knew that he was telling her he did not believe she loved Jeremy. Perhaps he was right ... but knowing that only whipped up her resentment and anger.

'What do you want me to do? Spend the rest of my life living alone without husband or children, all because I ...'

Just in time she stopped herself from completing what she had been about to say, too appalled by the words that had been on the tip of her tongue

to even be aware of the way Lucas was watching
her. 'Because I couldn't have you,' she had been
about to say, and she started to tremble, terrified
of the totally unexpected emotions her subconscious
had suddenly dredged up. 'You're being totally
unreasonable Lucas,' she said tiredly instead. 'You
haven't even met Jeremy yet and you know
nothing about him. I'm sorry if my being here is
an inconvenience to you. Just say the word, and
I'll pack and go. I had thought after all this time
we could perhaps as least talk civilly to one
another, but it seems I was wrong.' She turned
away from him and bent down to pick up her
case.

'I'll leave you to make my excuses to Gwendolin,
although I don't expect she wanted me here any
more than you do.'

'I'm quite sure you're right,' he mocked
sardonically, 'Or at least you would be if Gwen
still lived here.'

Lindsay's head shot up, her eyes rounding in
stunned amazement as she stared at him. 'She . . .'

'She and I decided to go our separate ways
shortly after Christmas,' Lucas told her curtly.
'The divorce came through several weeks ago.'

Lindsay felt so shaken that she subsided on to
her bed, her case forgotten. '*You* and Gwendolin
are *divorced* . . .' she shook her head, unable to
comprehend what he was saying. 'But why . . . why
didn't you let me know . . . why . . .'

Lucas shrugged powerful shoulders, turning his
back on her as he replied hardily. 'Why should I?
There was never any love lost between the pair of
you, and besides my marriage is hardly your
concern is it?'

Angry colour flamed hotly in Lindsay's face. 'You are my brother, Lucas,' she reminded him stiffly, only to be corrected with his soft answer.

'Stepbrother ... there's no real tie between us Lindsay, you know that.'

Lindsay decided to ignore his pointed gibe and instead said huskily, 'But you and Gwen ... I can hardly believe it ...'

'Oh I don't think I believe that. Gwen made her dissatisfaction with our marriage plain enough I always thought. The man she went away with wasn't her first lover.'

So Gwen had left him! Odd, she had never thought of that happening. Gwen had been so determined to marry him ... so obvious in her desire for him that Lindsay could not believe that she had actually been the one to be unfaithful. And Lucas ... he had married Gwen after all, so why should she be so surprised because he sounded so hurt and bitter. He must have cared for her. Just because *she* did not care for Gwen it did not follow that Lucas had not done so ... quite the contrary; after all he had married her; and was apparently so bitterly unhappy about their divorce that he was losing weight, the bitterly cynical streak in him increasingly marked.

He moved suddenly wrenching off his tie, and thrusting open the top buttons of his shirt. For a moment he looked so tired and defenceless that Lindsay's soft heart ached. He was still after all the same Lucas whom she so admired and worshipped ...

'You look tired.' The soft, sympathetic words were out before she could stop them. Lucas grimaced faintly but made no attempt to respond with the bitter mockery she had come to expect. 'Transatlantic flight does have that effect.' He ran a hand through his hair. 'Where the devil's Mrs James?'

'She's left you a note,' Lindsay told him. 'Apparently her sister's ill and she's needed to nurse her.'

'Hell!' Lucas swore explosively. 'I've got an American client coming over at the end of the week for a business meeting. I had intended to put him up here. We desperately need to secure a contract with him . . .'

'Is the business in difficulties then?' Lindsay was instantly worried.

'Not to any extent that will jeopardise your inheritance, if that's what's worrying you.' Lucas gave her a sour smile. 'It's just that last year we invested in some pretty expensive re-equipping that will pay off in the long run, but which has left us short of working capital for the present. We're still making enough profit to provide a skimming of butter on our bread, but the American contract would guarantee the jam . . . Worried that I might abscond with your inheritance Lindsay and that your blue-blooded suitor might reject you?'

He sounded so bitter that Lindsay was puzzled. Lucas knew the terms of her father's will as well as she did herself, but surely he knew her better than to believe she would marry simply to get her hands on her inheritance? The money did not matter in the slightest to her; no, what concerned her was her own sense of loyalty and duty to her father's wishes—old-fashioned perhaps, but then that was how she had been brought up, and yes, it hurt that Lucas should not know without her having to say it in so many words, why she was committing herself to marriage with Jeremy.

'No, Lucas,' she told him levelly at last. 'I obviously have more faith and trust in your sense of honour than you do in mine. I'll pack my things and leave,' she added, getting up off the bed and reaching for her case.'

'No.' His denial was forceful and sharp. 'It's too late for you to set off back to town at this time of evening,' he told her when she looked at him. 'You might as well stay now you're here.' He rubbed long fingers over the dark stubble on his jaw. 'I'd better go and grab a shower and a shave. I was on my way to do so when I heard the shower running in here. I thought for a moment that someone had broken in.'

'And having done so was taking a shower?' Lindsay's eyebrows rose, her irrepressible sense of fun bringing a smile to her lips, but Lucas didn't respond with a smile of his own. Instead his eyes changed from charcoal to black, smouldering darkly into her own before he turned on his heel and left her room.

CHAPTER THREE

FOR a long time after Lucas had gone, Lindsay simply stood, staring out of her bedroom window. Gwendolin and Lucas were divorced; it seemed almost impossible to believe. Almost as impossible as believing that Gwen had been the one to stray ... to take a lover ... no, lovers, if Lucas was to be believed. But why? She had never liked the older woman, but she had recognised her fiercely intense desire for Lucas.

Frowning slightly Lindsay withdrew from the window, suddenly becoming aware of the chilly breeze and the thinness of her robe. As she walked towards the wardrobe, the mirror on the dressing table threw back her reflection and she grimaced faintly. The thin robe clung silkily to her skin, outlining the full curves of her breasts, following the indentation of her waist and then the narrow out-thrust of her hips. Disturbed by her own inner awareness of her sexuality she dressed hurriedly. Lucas had not proved over-receptive to the news of her engagement; in fact he had been almost brutal in his mockery of it. Her chin tilted proudly. Yes, it was true in some respects that without her father's money Jeremy would not want to marry her, but that was not something she did not already know. What did Lucas want her to do? she wondered wrathfully. Fall in love with someone totally unsuitable just so that he could have the pleasure of pointing

out her folly to her and reminding her of her
father's wishes?

Of course it was only natural that Lucas should
be bitter and angry at Gwendolin's desertion, but
why take it out on *her*? She would have plenty of
opportunity to talk to him over dinner, she
reminded herself, wishing again that Jeremy had
been able to accompany her. If Lucas could see
and talk to Jeremy himself he would realise the
rightness of her decision. Perhaps there was no
excitement or deeply intense emotion in her
relationship with Jeremy, but there was liking and
mutual respect that would build a good life
together. Sexual chemistry was all very well in its
way, but Lindsay wasn't sure if she would trust
such volatile emotions. Startlingly, for the first
time it struck her that the reason she might never
have experienced intense physical desire was
because she had deliberately programmed herself
against doing so. She could remember quite vividly
the feeling of self disgust and shame she had
experienced when Gwendolin had accused her of
wanting Lucas as a man and not as a brother. Her
seventeen year old self had been shocked by the
older woman's vitriolic claim and had instantly
denied it, but she could not deny that Lucas was
an extremely attractive man. Even just now,
despite his bitter anger, she had sensed the
magnetic pull of his personality; the heady,
breathless sensation of no longer being quite in
control of herself or her reactions.

She was here to inform Lucas of her impending
engagement, not to daydream about the past, she
reminded herself severely, opening her wardrobe
and surveying the clothes she had brought with

her. She had come prepared for all contingencies, knowing Gwendolin's love of entertaining, but it seemed hardly appropriate to wear an evening dress simply to dine with Lucas. She frowned over a tweed skirt and toning silk shirt, dismissing them as not dressy enough and eventually decided on the soft lilac Jean Muir dress she had owned for several seasons and which remained a firm favourite, the excellence of the fabric and its cut ensuring that it was suitable for a whole host of occasions.

The colour suited her, emphasising the delicacy of her pale English complexion, the long lean line of the dress with its swing of pleats from the hip, comfortable and yet at the same time subtly feminine. Brushing her hair thoroughly she secured it in a loose chignon, on impulse putting in her ears the pearl and diamond studs which had been Lucas' eighteenth birthday present to her. She wasn't wearing Jeremy's ring. He wanted to present it to her formally next weekend when they went to visit his parents but for some reason tonight she would have welcomed its presence on her finger. Why? Because she felt that wearing it might convince Lucas of the rightness of their engagement. She didn't need his permission to marry she reminded herself ... Jeremy was everything her father had wanted for her in a husband. Sighing faintly she sprayed her wrists lightly with perfume and then remembering the housekeeper's absence, decided that if they were to eat dinner, she'd better go downstairs and see about preparing it.

In the event there wasn't a good deal of preparation necessary. The housekeeper had left everything ready in the fridge, and all Lindsay was required to do was to heat it up in the oven. She was a good cook who enjoyed exercising her skill. When she was married to Jeremy she felt sure she would have plenty of opportunity to do so. He would not want her to work; he had already told her that much and when, as was eventually planned, he took over the running of the estate from his father, she would have plenty to occupy her time. Until then she would be expected to occupy herself preparing clever little dinner parties for Jeremy's friends and clients, shopping ... gossiping ... having children. It was the accepted mode of wifely behaviour amongst Jeremy's set.

It seemed silly when there was just the two of them for them to dine formally in the vastness of the dining room, so instead Lindsay placed cutlery and glasses on the much smaller table of the little breakfast room just off the kitchen. She had always liked this room which caught the early morning sun and although Gwen had completely altered the decor and furnishings, standing by the window observing the view she had observed so often as a child, brought back a stream of half-submerged memories.

'Wondering how you can get your own way?'

She hadn't heard Lucas come in, and she turned tensely at the sound of his voice, instantly aware of the clean male scent of him ... of the fact that his hair was still faintly damp from his shower, and that his body, beneath its civilised sheath of sophisticated clothes, moved with all the predatory grace of the hunter.

'No ... as a matter of fact, I was remembering how I fell in the lake the year I was twelve, and how you fished me out.'

It was no less than the truth, and just for a moment his mouth softened slightly and she was almost able to persuade herself that he was once again the old Lucas whom she had loved so much ... and who, she had once thought, loved her in return.

'Yes ... You don't know how close you came to being walloped. You'd been expressly forbidden to ride your bike along the lake path.'

The bike in question—a brand new two wheeler had been a birthday present and she had desperately wanted to try it out. It had been raining heavily for several days though and the lakeside path had been dangerously muddy. She had known all this, but still she had defied Lucas' suggestion that she wait to try the bike until he could go with her. She had paid for her defiance with a thorough soaking and a bad fright ... Lucas had been furious ... she remembered grimacing faintly, and she could well remember sensing how angry he was with her. But he had taught her to ride ... and then she had known instinctively that beneath the anger there was a deep vein of caring. Where had it all gone?

'Dinner's ready,' she told him, forcing herself back to the present. 'If you sit down I'll go and get it for you.'

'Buttering me up, Lindsay?' he asked unpleasantly, and then as though sensing her lack of comprehension he added drily. 'I'm not used to being waited on these days. Dinner is normally a meal I manage to grab somewhere between 'phone calls. No doubt in the ordered household you intend to run after your marriage, things will be very different. Why are you marrying him, Lindsay?'

He sounded so derisive that she almost lost her own temper. 'Because I want to.' She held his gaze levelly, and then asked softly, 'What do you expect me to say Lucas? Because we're madly in love with one another? I can't pretend to emotions I don't feel, but I can honestly say that I don't trust that sort of sexual fascination . . . it dies . . . and I don't believe it to be a good foundation for an enduring marriage . . .'

'And you of course, have a vast wealth of experience,' he mocked her suddenly savage in the way he looked and sounded. His fingers closed painfully round her wrist as he yanked her round so that the light from the window fell sharply across her pale face. 'Just how often have you experienced sexual desire to be able to talk so knowledgeably about it Lindsay? How often have you been savaged by the sharp teeth of frustration . . . How often have you lain alone in bed at night, burning up with the need for another human being.'

His savagery took her by surprise, and it was several seconds before she realised he had misinterpreted her remarks as a criticism of his motives in marrying Gwen. For some reason it hurt her to think of him hurting . . . wanting the wife who no longer, apparently wanted him. Almost instinctively she lifted her hand to his face, offering the age-old gesture of comfort and compassion, but he jerked back before she could touch him, rage burning in the blackness of his eyes.

'For God's sake let's eat,' he said thickly, 'or is

starvation another of the ploys you intend to use against me, Lindsay?'

His cynicism both hurt and angered her, but as she served their meal, Lindsay reminded herself that he too had been hurt; that losing Gwen was obviously the reason behind his behaviour. It was strange in a way for, although he had married her, in the past Lindsay had never witnessed any intimacy or emotion between them that could have led her to expect his present grief. In fact had anyone asked her she would have said that of the two of them Gwendolin was the one who cared the most. Patently she had been wrong, but then she had been wrong about Lucas so many times already that should hardly surprise her.

Dinner was an almost silent meal. Lucas seemed morose, sunk in his own thoughts. He checked every attempt she made to introduce the subject of her engagement. Perhaps it was crass of her to want to discuss it now when he had just told her of his own divorce, but Jeremy was a man who once his plans were made, hated any change being made in them. If she had returned to London with the subject of her engagement undiscussed, Jeremy would no doubt have felt obliged to put off the official announcement to his parents and family which was planned for next weekend.

She tried to explain a little of this to Lucas, but all he did was to grimace bitterly and enquire with heavy sarcasm. 'If that's the case, how come he isn't here seeking my permission to pay his addresses to you.'

His sarcasm was the last straw. Lindsay could feel temper igniting inside her and although she fought against it, it overpowered her. Pushing aside her half-eaten meal she stood up, her skin pink with angry colour, her eyes glowing hot gold as she stared across the table at Lucas.

'Perhaps because you are not my guardian and nor do I need your permission to marry,' she threw at him angrily.

'But you do need my approval to your choice of prospective husband before you can inherit under the terms of your father's will,' Lucas pointed out to her with maddening accuracy. His mouth twisted slightly as he added, 'And don't tell me, as I know you're dying to, that he'll marry you, fortune or not, because we both know it isn't true, don't we, Lindsay? For God's sake why don't you find yourself a man who doesn't give a damn about your father's money; who wants you for yourself and is satisfied with you alone? Or are you frightened that such a man doesn't exist.' He too was standing now, towering over her as he placed his hands on the table, gripping the polished wood, anger, bitterness and something else turning his grey eyes smoky charcoal as he watched the effect his words were having on her. 'Is that why you're so keen to be an obedient daughter and do what daddy wanted Lindsay? Is it because you feel so damned inadequate ... because ...' He had closed the distance between them and was shaking her now ... quite hard. Lindsay could feel the savage imprint of his fingers against the fragile bones of her shoulders; just as she could feel the rage he was suppressing. It wasn't fair ... why should he take his bitterness and anger out on her ... why should he be able to say such cruel things to her.

'Is that it Lindsay?' he demanded thickly, holding her eyes with his own. 'Is it ...?'

The fierce savagery in his voice, broke the spell his touch had sealed her in. Anger rose up inside her, destroying all her old inhibitions. Her voice was thick with tears, her vision of him blurring as shamingly they stormed her eyes. 'No damn you it isn't ...' she raised her hand initially to brush them away, but the look of sardonic comprehension informing his eyes made her change her mind, and acting on an impulse she had never experienced before she lashed out at him, more shocked herself than he was by the livid imprint her palm left along his lean cheek, and the thick silence that followed the delivery of her impulsive blow.

Lucas released her immediately, his mouth curling mockingly as he saw the way she flinched back.

He shook his head and said softly, 'Oh no Lindsay, I'm not going to hit you back much as you might deserve it.' A humourless smile curled his mouth. 'If I were you, right now I'd not be worrying too much about what I'd done, but I would be wondering why? Was it because you couldn't endure to hear the truth? And it is the truth Lindsay ... Have you and ... Jeremy ever made love?'

The sudden change in his line of questioning stunned her momentarily and then pride came to her rescue. Forcing a light, cool laugh she said quietly. 'Really Lucas ... is that any of your business?'

'Perhaps not,' he agreed, 'but you'll tell me anyway, won't you?'

He was doing it again ... almost mesmerising her with the intense concentration of his attention, forcing her to weaken and give way to him, but she was not going to do so. Turning away from him she walked to the door, facing him only once she was there. 'I'm going to my room, Lucas,' she told him quietly. 'I can see no profit to either of us in continuing our present discussion. Tomorrow morning I'll go home . . .'

'Without having my approval?' His voice taunted her, but she held on to her temper.

'If you really intend to withhold your approval then I'll have to consult daddy's solicitor. He knows the terms of the will as well as you do yourself, and I'm sure he'll agree with me that in this case you're being unfair and unreasonable.'

'Blackmail, Lindsay?' She watched the way his mouth twisted, dark bitterness invading his eyes. 'You must want him one hell of a lot. Perhaps I misjudged you and you do love him after all. Tell me honestly that you love and want him to the extent that life without him would be totally insupportable.'

Just for a moment she was tempted to do just that, but the deep rooted inner honesty that had proved so troublesome to her as a teenager raised its head now and would not let her. 'I like and respect him,' she said calmly, 'and I believe that together we'll have a pleasant and rewarding life, but no, I don't love him as you're defining the word Lucas.'

It seemed impossible that that could actually be relief she saw flaring in his eyes—impossible indeed when they hardened cruelly and he taunted, 'You're a coward Lindsay . . .'

Anger overwhelmed her again. 'And if I am,' she stormed back at him. 'Aren't you partially to blame? I haven't forgotten how eager you were to marry me off when my father died, Lucas . . . and don't tell me it was my welfare that motivated you . . . You simply wanted me off your hands and out of your life because you wanted to marry Gwen. You were eager enough then for me to comply with the terms of my father's will. Perhaps if I had met someone I could love as you define love, things might have been different,' she admitted honestly, 'but I have not done so . . . In fact I don't believe I'm capable of experiencing that sort of love . . .'

She didn't think he was listening to her. He had turned to face the window and had his back to her and from the tension holding his body tensely rigid she suspected that her casual reference to his marriage had stirred up memories and anguish that were causing him so much pain that he was barely aware of her presence any longer. Quietly slipping from the room, as she headed upstairs she reflected on the maelstrom of emotions she seemed to have plunged into since her arrival. Lucas had obviously loved Gwendolin far more intensely than she had ever suspected. He was not a man who openly betrayed his emotions, at least not normally. She certainly had never seen him so angry or bitter before. An alien quiver of sensation ran through her body, and she halted suddenly up the stairs, remembering the cool hard feel of his skin beneath her palm; the response that had flashed momentarily in his eyes as she hit him, and the exhilerating dangerous sensation she had experienced as their mutual anger exploded. No man had ever provoked such feelings inside her before.

More slowly this time she continued on her way upstairs, closing the door of her bedroom behind her. It was too early for her to go to bed yet, but she did not want to go back downstairs and risk further arguments with Lucas. Had she really meant it when she had threatened to go to the family solicitor . . .? Did she really want to marry Jeremy so much that she was prepared to defy Lucas to do so? It wasn't so much Jeremy, she admitted to herself, when she had thought about it . . . it was the fact that she knew Lucas was being both unreasonable and unfair. Jeremy was everything her father had wanted for her in a husband. She liked him . . . they understood one another, but Lucas was deliberately trying to foster doubts in her mind . . . Why?

Restlessly she prowled round her room, her eye falling on her old bookcase. Her books were still in it, and she smiled slightly remembering the many hours of pleasure they had given her. Here was her first book of 'grown-up' poems. Lucas had given it to her on her thirteenth birthday. She extracted the slim leather bound volume from the case, opening it slowly. 'To Lindsay on her thirteenth birthday, from Lucas, with my love,' he had written inside. How she had treasured those words. She hadn't shown the book to any of her friends she remembered a trifle wryly. It had been too precious for that. Her father had given her a new pony. She had kissed him enthusiastically she remembered, all the time conscious of Lucas' grey gaze upon her. She had kissed Sheila too . . . but when it had been Lucas' turn to be thanked for his gift, she had felt awkward and embarrassed. In the end he had been the one to kiss her . . . a brotherly peck on her cheek, but if she closed her eyes she could still remember the pounding excitement of her heart because his arms were round her, his body close to hers.

Lindsay closed the book with a sharp snap replacing it in the bookcase. Strange how until now she had forgotten that small incident . . . had forgotten how ambivalent her feelings towards Lucas had been as she entered her teens. She had loved and adored him as her brother of course, but there had been other feelings inextricably entwined with those fraternal ones . . . budding sensations and emotions she had found it hard to cope with . . . sensations so alien to those she felt she ought to be feeling that she had buried them deep inside herself, refusing to admit to them. It seemed both ridiculous and childish now . . . looking back from the security of twenty-four she could see nothing shameful in her budding emotional response to Lucas. He had always been and still was a very attractive member of the male species, and it was no wonder really that her newly emergent femininity had responded so overwhelmingly to his presence.

She had felt so guilty, she remembered now . . . so mixed up about her feelings, but there had been no one she could turn to talk about them. Strange how she had all but forgotten how she had felt. She must have buried her reactions so deeply that it had taken this evening's highly charged emotional scene to bring them to mind again.

If Sheila had not been Lucas' mother, no doubt she could have talked to her, and Sheila, sensible and kind woman that she was would doubtless have explained and reassured her that what she was experiencing was a perfectly normal part of growing up, but she had been too shy and ashamed to confide in anyone. At thirteen she was well aware of her father's plans for her and knew quite well that those plans did not include Lucas. He of course at that time had a regular procession of girlfriends in and out of his life. She could vividly remember one of them ... a leggy, pretty redhead, whom she had discovered him kissing one evening when Shelia and her father were out. She had been upstairs in bed, but she hadn't been able to sleep. She had gone downstairs for a drink. The sitting room door had been open, the light from the hall shining directly on to the embracing couple on the settee. Lucas had seen her first, transfixed like a moth by the light as she stood in that beam of light unable to tear her fascinated, horrified gaze away.

She remembered now how much she had trembled as he came towards her, her senses relaying to her the male scent of his body ... the knowledge outside her own experience and yet known to her through some deep rooted feminine awareness that he was sexually aroused. Shock and fascination both had been inextricably woven together. She had expected his anger, but he had been quietly gentle with her, calming her, she now realised as he might have done a nervous animal, asking what she was doing downstairs, whilst from the sitting room his girlfriend's querulous voice demanded his return. She remembered her ignominious flight back to her room, and how the next day and for several days afterward she had studiedly ignored all Lucas' attempts to talk to her. A briefly reminiscent smile curved her mouth,

as she recalled her teenage air of affronted dignity
and aloofness. All caused by jealousy of course.
Jealous? Lindsay frowned over her adult analysis
of her teenage emotions. Had she been jealous? Of
course she had, her adult self told her, and quite
naturally so ... She had been jealous both as a
sister and as a budding woman ... Still frowning
Lindsay leaned on her open window, deliberately
forcing herself to go back through those teenage
years and to study them now with the knowledge
of experience. Of course it would have been
inevitable that she should have had a mild crush
on Lucas, deny it to Gwen though she might—but
the older woman had been deliberately cruel in
revealing her own weakness to her, Lindsay
thought. A woman with more compassion would
have seen the truth, but would not have used it as
a weapon. Teenage emotions are so tender and
vulnerable, teenagers so intensely open to pain ...
and she had been hurt ... both by Gwen and then
by Lucas, when he had tried to persuade her into
marriage. Sighing faintly Lindsay decided she
might as well go to bed. It was sad really when she
thought of all that she and Lucas had lost. They
had once been so close, and, she acknowledged
now, it was the pain of losing that closeness
that had made her so suspicious of adult
love. She had lost Lucas as a teenager and the
memory of the pain that had caused her had made
her withdraw into herself. Could it perhaps be the
scorching jealousy and bitter shame she had felt
when she saw Lucas with another woman in his
arms that had helped to make her so cold sexually?
It was a new and startling thought. It would be
wrong to blame Lucas for all her own inadequacies

she told herself sternly, and yet there was no point in denying to herself that there had been a time when she had experienced all the fierce pangs of teenage desire, and Lucas had been the one she desired. If she concentrated hard enough she could even remember how she had felt . . . how much she had actually ached for him to kiss her as she had seen him kissing that red-headed girl—and how ashamed of herself she had been because she felt that way. All water under the bridge now of course. She could see her teenage crush for exactly what it had been. But why was she remembering all this tonight, when for so many years she had kept it so deeply buried that she had refused to admit even to herself that she had felt that way?

She was on the eve of marriage, she reminded herself, about to take one of the most serious steps to commitment a human being could take and it was only natural that the emotional disturbance should activate old memories. Perhaps it was time they were resurrected anyway . . . time she gave the past a thorough spring-cleaning and discarded what was no longer needed. Had Lucas known how she felt? Maybe, maybe not—certainly the old Lucas would never have wanted to hurt her. Unlike Gwen, she thought frowning again. Why had Gwen hated her so much? Not because she had viewed her in the light of a rival. Lucas had never seen her as anything more than a sister, Lindsay was ready to swear to that. Perhaps it had simply been that Gwen had not been able to bear sharing him with anyone.

If that had been the case, where had it gone, all that fierce emotion and possessiveness? Poor Lucas . . . it was no wonder really that he had been

so savage with her. Regret and compassion
softened her earlier anger towards him. Their
quarrel seemed so silly and pointless now.
Impulsively Lindsay got up and pulled her robe on
over her thin silk nightdress. She would go
downstairs and talk to Lucas again . . . calmly this
time . . . She would make him see how right this
marriage was for her . . . and this time she would
not antagonise him . . . She could not simply leave
in the morning with the knowledge that they had
quarrelled and parted on bad terms still behind
her. It was still quite early. Only eleven o'clock
and Lucas, she knew kept late hours.

The landing light was off, but Lindsay knew her
way so well that she did not need it. Besides a bold
hunter's moon threw ghostly patches of light in
through the tall windows. Pausing at the head of
the stairs, Lindsay glanced automatically in the
direction of Lucas' room. Light shone under his
bedroom door. She frowned slightly, checking . . .
perhaps he had come to bed after all. She hesitated
for a moment, chewing on her bottom lip, and
then knowing that sleep would be impossible if she
did not speak to him she walked determinedly
towards his door, and knocked briefly on it before
entering.

At one time his bedroom had been as familiar
to her as her own, but of course, Gwen had
changed the decor completely. It came as quite a
shock therefore to see in the illumination of the
bedside lamp that the vivid red and black colour
scheme she had favoured had vanished to be
replaced with a much more masculine navy and
white decor. Her heart ached for Lucas when she
realised that after Gwen had left him, unable to

bear the memories he must have have the entire room changed.

'Lindsay?'

The curtness in his voice reminded her of the way they had parted. He was standing by the door to his bathroom, wearing a towelling robe.

'I had to talk to you Lucas.' Heavens how tremulous and soft her voice sounded, almost unfamiliarly so. She could sense Lucas' restrained impatience and heard the sigh in his voice as he asked, 'Why *now*, Lindsay? Why couldn't it wait until morning?'

She shrugged slightly, feeling a little uncomfortable. What could she say, that wouldn't sound silly? She could hardly tell him that their quarrel had made it impossible for her to sleep . . . that the old memories she herself had stirred up had made her ache for the closeness they had once shared . . . for his affection and approval. If she did he would probably only laugh at her.

'Poor little Lindsay,' he suddenly mocked her, breaking into her train of thought. 'Daren't you go back and tell him I haven't agreed? Are you frightened he won't marry you without my approval Lindsay? Why does that worry you? Is he such a good lover that you can't bear to lose him?'

Subduing an impulse to tell him that she and Jeremy had never been lovers, Lindsay asked instead, 'Why is it you're so against my engagement Lucas? Why?'

He took his time in answering her, walking towards her and stopping when he was only feet away. 'Perhaps because it seems so inhuman and calculated.' His mouth twisted in what was fast becoming familiar bitterness. 'Have you never

wondered what it would be like to feel real
emotion Lindsay to want a man with your heart
and soul as well as with your body?'

'Lucas. . . .' She took an involuntary step
toward him, touching the bare, hair darkened flesh
of his arm with nervous fingertips, and wishing she
hadn't when he instantly recoiled from her.

'Go back to your own room, Lindsay.' His voice
was harsh with anger, the force of it shocking her.

'Why . . . what . . .'

'Look I can't talk to you whilst you're dressed,
or rather undressed like that.' He looked grimly at
her, making her acutely conscious of the flimsiness
of her silk nightdress and its matching robe. Her
whole body had started to tremble in open
reaction to his words and to protect herself from
them she said huskily, 'Lucas you're my brother
I . . .'

'Your stepbrother,' he grated correcting her.
'Your stepbrother Lindsay that's all . . . there's no
blood tie between us; no law either temporal or
ecclesiastical which prevents me from responding to
the provocation you're offering.'

Provocation? Lindsay stared at him, but he
seemed to be lost in his own emotions and
bitterness, his eyes, she was sure, not seeing her,
but dark with pain caused no doubt by the loss of
his wife. 'Is that why you came in here Lindsay?'
he demanded harshly. 'Because you hoped to
persuade me by other means than words to agree
to your engagement . . .'

'No, no. Lucas . . . how could you think that?'
Shock made her voice shake nervously. 'Lucas, I
know you must be missing Gwen, but . . .'

'But I mustn't misinterpret the reasons for

your being in my room ... I mustn't give rein to the feelings the sight of you wearing next to nothing arouses in my frustrated body ... is that it Lindsay? Well why the hell not,' he added in a thick mutter. 'Just why the hell not.'

His arms, binding her against his body felt so familiar that she could not believe he had not held her like this a thousand times before. The touch of his hands as they slid beneath the silk of her robe to stroke and caress the bare skin of her shoulders so pleasurable that she couldn't even think of restraining him. Instead she let herself melt into him, raising her face instinctively for his kiss, her mouth parting wantonly beneath the insistent pressure of his, everything else forgotten as he shaped her body to his, kissing her with a deep famished hunger that fired her senses, unleashing all the emotions she had thought herself incapable of feeling, making her body ache deliriously. His hand touched her breast and she shuddered deeply aware of her own instant response, aware that Lucas was muttering her name with raw urgency that did nothing to damp down her rioting senses, his mouth hot, burning into her skin as it caressed the silky flesh of her throat. Somehow her own hands had found their way inside his robe and were shaping the hard muscles of his chest, glorying in their freedom to do so. It was all so instinctively right ... pleasure exploded inside her shaking her with its force, happiness so intense that it was almost unbearable, and then suddenly Lucas was pushing her away and reality came thundering in. This time when she shuddered it was with shame and agony instead of pleasure. Unable to even look at him she fled from the room.

Alone in her own bed she forced herself to relive

the incident. Why had it happened now of all times? Lucas' behaviour was easy to explain. He had told her quite openly that he was suffering from sexual frustration and in his anger he had been able to deceive himself that she had deliberately set out to arouse him, but her own response to him ... her own emotions ... these were far harder to explain. All she could think was that somehow the past had, for a few mad seconds become woven with the present and that she had kissed and wanted him not as the woman she now was, but as the girl she had once been. That could be the only explanation ... it had to be the only explanation. Feeling a little calmer she composed herself for sleep. Tomorrow morning she would leave, she decided firmly. She would go back to London, and if Lucas continued to oppose her engagement then she would just, as she had already threatened, have to appeal to the family solicitor. She closed her eyes, refusing to allow herself to remember the touch of Lucas' mouth against her own ... his hands on her body ... and willed herself instead to think of Jeremy, but somehow the thought of him touching and caressing her as Lucas had just done aroused no emotion inside her other than a mild sense of revulsion. Reaction, she reassured herself tiredly ... reaction that's all it was, nothing more ... Just delayed adolescent reaction.

CHAPTER FOUR

THE moment she opened her eyes Lindsay knew that she had overslept; the position of the sun shining through her window at an unfamiliar level told her that much and a brief glance at her watch confirmed it. Groaning slightly she got up and hurried into her bathroom. She had wanted to be up and away early—so early that if possible she could avoid seeing Lucas.

Lucas . . . her face and body flamed with hot colour as she remembered the previous evening. Had he known how eagerly and shamelessly she had gone into his arms? Very probably . . . after all he was hardly inexperienced.

Dressing with feverish haste Lindsay flung her clothes into her suitcase, pausing to reflect on how much had happened in the short space of time since she had unpacked it.

Her stomach churning far too violently to permit her to even think of eating any breakfast, Lindsay nevertheless decided that she would be wise to at least make herself a drink.

The kitchen was empty, the whole house almost uncannily silent. She made herself a cup of coffee, forcing herself to sip it slowly instead of gulping it down, every muscle in her body tensed in dread of Lucas' arrival, and yet conversely some part of her was disappointed when he did not materialise. Her coffee drunk and her cup washed there was nothing to prevent her departure and yet, for some reason she felt unwilling to go. Sighing in faint exasperation at her own unfamiliar indecision, Lindsay went back upstairs to get her case. As she walked past Lucas' room she noticed that the door was slightly open, but resolutely she refused to look. She was past the door when she heard the noise, faint and indistinct, but chilling nonetheless as she took in its implications. Lucas was still in his room and moreover he was talking to someone!

Against all the urgings of her mind, Lindsay stopped. Had Gwendolin perhaps come back? Why should she? She and Lucas were divorced, not separated, Lindsay reminded herself, and yet who else could Lucas be talking to in that low voiced intimate mutter, in the privacy of his bedroom at this time of the morning?

Suddenly, shockingly, as she stood there, Lindsay heard her own name, muttered with compellingly sharp clarity, and like someone in a dream she moved toward the open door.

The closed curtains gave the room a sombre dimness and it took several seconds for Lindsay's eyes to adjust to the lack of daylight. Lucas was still in bed. She could see the naked, golden curve of his back, and her stomach muscles knotted agonisingly as he suddenly turned over, rumpling the already disordered bed. Almost choked by the ferocity of her heartbeats Lindsay waited for him to make some scathing comment, and then realised that his eyes were still closed and that he was apparently still asleep. He muttered something unintelligible, pushing away the bedclothes, and icy fingers of fear danced along her spine as Lindsay saw the dark, hectic fever flush colouring his skin. Without allowing herself time to think she went over to the bed, and reached out a tentative hand to touch his skin. It burned against her own, fever-hot and again Lindsay felt a surge of fear. Lucas was ill . . . and the conversation she had thought she had heard had been the ramblings of a sick man.

Beneath her hand his forehead burned, a thick lock of dark hair brushing silkily against her fingers as he moved feverishly beneath her touch. She would have to ring the doctor . . . Lindsay had seen Lucas like this twice before and knew that he was suffering from a recurrence of a tropical fever he had picked up as a small child. His father had worked out in Africa for several years, and Lucas and his mother had lived there with him until Lucas had contracted this fever and their doctor had advised that he return home. Lindsay knew all this from Sheila, just as she knew that when Lucas was subject to one of his fortunately rare, recurrent bouts of illness, the only cure was time and rest, plus a course of antibiotics. The previous two attacks which she had witnessed had occurred at times when Lucas had been under considerable stress, and she wondered if this present one perhaps had its roots in his divorce.

Anxious to have medical confirmation that she was right in her diagnosis, Lindsay ran downstairs to the study, quickly finding and dialling the doctor's number. She was lucky enough to catch him in just before he set out on his rounds, and when she described Lucas' condition, he promised that he would be round as soon as he could.

'In the meantime, sponge him down if you can manage it—that will bring his temperature down a little bit, and if you can manage to get any fluid inside him ... Mrs James will help you with that ...'

Doctor Simmonds had been their family doctor all through Lindsay's childhood, and she felt no qualms in telling him about Mrs James' absence.

'Umm ... well it's lucky for Lucas that you happened to be there,' was his only comment.

Sponge Lucas down the doctor had told her, and Lindsay felt an odd quivering seize hold of her muscles as she contemplated carrying out such an intimate task.

'Stop being so Victorian,' she chided herself ruthlessly as she went back upstairs. 'Until last night you were quite happy to see Lucas as your brother ... so why go all dithery and nervous now? Why? Because since then Lucas had kissed and touched her, and in doing so had wakened her to facets of her own personality and emotions she had hitherto successfully concealed from herself; *that* was why, Lindsay admitted wryly to herself. It seemed ironic that Lucas should be able to arouse in her feelings that Jeremy for all his suitability as a husband could not.

Back upstairs, she hesitated outside Lucas' room, and then reminding herself firmly that he was a sick man and as such in need of her care and help she went in.

Lucas obviously hadn't moved since she left him. He was lying on his back breathing heavily, his skin still darkly flushed, perspiration dampening his skin. The bedclothes had slipped down to his waist and when Lindsay tentatively touched his chest it was hot to her touch. He was sweating profusely, the bedclothes around him damp, the dark arrowing of body hair on his chest slick with moisture. As she stood uncertainly beside the bed he opened his eyes, the dark lashes glued spikily together, his gaze dark and blind as he muttered in a hoarse, unfamiliar voice, 'We have to get that contract . . . we need it . . . do you hear me?'

Sensing that he was oblivious to her presence and gripped completely by his fever-induced thoughts, Lindsay soothed him automatically, talking in a soft, low voice, which seemed to work because he stopped muttering and closed his eyes again. These ramblings had been a feature of his illness when he had succumbed to the fever before, she remembered, and she frowned a little recalling that on one occasion the fever had been bought on by the strain of working for his finals when he was at Oxford. Then she remembered he had raved about his exams, going over and over the questions he had been set. Now he seemed to be concerned about some contract, and her stomach muscles clenched tensely. Was there some problem with the business? Something he had not told her fully the previous evening when they were discussing it?

'Lindsay.'

The husky, but quite lucid tone in which he said her name brought her out of her thoughts. Her eyes went immediately to his, expecting to see him looking at her calmly, but instead his eyes were still tightly closed.

He said her name again, this time in a hoarse mutter, and reacting instinctively, Lindsay bent down to touch him. 'It's all right Lucas, I'm here,' she told him softly, surprised to feel the tension which had gripped his body when she touched him, suddenly easing.

'Don't go away ... stay with me ...'

He must have got her confused with Gwen, Lindsay thought wryly. The Lucas she knew would never ask for her company. He had already made it plain it was the last thing he wanted, but the mere fact that he had said her name; that he had betrayed a need to her, made it easier for her to go into his bathroom and return with a damp sponge and a towel.

Touching him, however, without being aware of him as a man was not so easy, and it was only by tensing every muscle and reminding herself that he was ill and that she was engaged to someone else—or virtually so, that she was able to carry out her task. The coolness of the sponge seemed to soothe him slightly because his movements became less restless and when Lindsay returned from the bathroom with a fresh towel he seemed to have drifted into a more natural sleep. Watching him she had a cowardly impulse to leave him alone and to go downstairs to await Doctor Simmonds arrival, but even as the thought formed, Lucas started to twist restlessly again, fresh beads of sweat springing up on his body.

Sighing faintly Lindsay started to re-sponge his chest, appalled by the storm of sensation touching him aroused inside her. The mere act of touching him made her ache inside, so intensely that she could hardly believe this was actually her, experiencing these alien and exhausting emotions. She had just finished sponging Lucas down for the third time when she heard a car drawing up outside, and she reached the window just in time to see Doctor Simmonds climbing out.

Sighing in relief she hurried downstairs to let him in.

The last time she had seen him had been at Christmas when he and his wife had attended one of Gwen's many cocktail parties. Gwen was not particularly fond of the Simmondses, Lindsay remembered, but Lucas had been insistent on them being included.

Lindsay stayed downstairs whilst the Doctor went up to Lucas' room, busying herself making them both a cup of coffee. She heard him coming back down again and went into the hall to meet him.

'You were quite right,' he confirmed, accepting her offer of a drink and following her into the kitchen. 'It's a recurrence of his old fever—pretty bad this time too.' He frowned thoughtfully sipping his coffee. 'He only seems to suffer from it when he's under a considerable amount of pressure ... both emotional and physical ... I wonder what brought this attack on?'

It was Lindsay's turn to frown. 'Well, I expect losing Gwen and I know he's concerned about some contract or other. He was delirious earlier and he kept referring to it.'

'Yes. He did say the last time I saw him that he was hoping to get a new American contract, but Lucas is a tough and shrewd businessman, I shouldn't have thought that would have brought this on.'

'Not on its own perhaps,' Lindsay agreed, 'but coupled with losing Gwen ...'

'Good riddance if you ask me,' Doctor

Simmonds shocked her by saying rather unsympathetically. 'Never could see why he married her in the first place—apart from the obvious reason, and she'd already made it more than plain that he could have that without marriage—and nor would he have been the first,' he added, almost as though he sensed the shocked denial hovering on Lindsay's tongue.

'Now don't look like that my dear,' he counselled her with a brief smile. 'I might be past my best, but that doesn't mean I'm not aware of what goes on around me. Gwen made a deliberate set at Lucas from the moment she set eyes on him, and I for one was very disappointed in him when he married her, but then I suppose with your parents both dead, and no one else available, he felt that for your sake if nothing else, he should have a wife.' When he saw Lindsay's expression he grimaced slightly. 'People will talk my dear, and in truth as I remember it there were already tongues wagging even before he married Gwen. After all you were living together.'

'But Lucas is my stepbrother,' Lindsay murmured, stunned by what he was telling her. 'He never ... I ...'

'My dear, I know there was nothing in the rumours, and to be honest, I suspect that Gwen had a hand in circulating them ... after all it would have suited her purpose very nicely and added considerable weight to her case. Lucas always did take his responsibilities seriously, and he was I suppose, standing *in loco parentis* to you ...'

'You're surely not suggesting that Lucas married Gwen to protect me from rumours?'

'Not entirely, but I wouldn't entirely discount it as one of the reasons that might have motivated him. I must admit I wasn't surprised when I'd heard that they'd parted. I don't think she ever made him happy. I certainly noticed a change in him after you left. However, it's all water under the bridge now,' he concluded comfortably, adding, 'Will you be able to stay and look after him, or do you want to make arrangements to engage a private nurse? I warn you it could be a couple of weeks before he's properly on the mend.'

Lindsay stared at him. She had been so concerned with the immediacy of Lucas' illness that she hadn't thought any further ahead than the doctor's arrival ... Of course Lucas would need nursing; she should have thought of that. Her mind winged back to the past ... to the countless trays she had carried up to his room during his last convalescence ... How many hours had she spent with him then ... keeping him entertained, keeping him resting in bed when he had wanted to get up.

'I'll stay and take care of him.' The words were out and the commitment made before she could deny either, and she saw from the approving look Doctor Simmonds gave her that she had given him the response he had expected.

'Good girl ... I hoped you'd say that. That's the trouble with these healthy virile males—they make the most dreadful patients. Of course you'll probably get a better response from him than anyone else. He always did have a rather soft spot for you.'

'He did?' Lindsay couldn't help betraying a certain wry bitterness. What would Doctor

Simmonds say if she told him about their recent quarrel . . . and about Lucas' method of punishing her for her defiance?

Don't stay here, a cautioning inner voice warned her. Leave now and get a nurse to look after Lucas, but she knew she could not do that . . . She could not simply wipe away all the childhood memories and consign Lucas to someone else's care.

Doctor Simmonds was already getting up and Lindsay knew it was too late to take back her offer. 'I'll get a prescription made up for you and drop it round this afternoon. You'll have to keep sponging him down whilst the fever's at its height—he's a strong lad, it shouldn't be for too long. The antibiotics I'm going to give you should start working pretty quickly. Your main problem is going to be getting fluids into him—he'll probably fight you,' he warned Lindsay, 'but it is essential that you get him to drink as much as possible, especially while the fever's at its height. Think you can cope?'

Here was her chance to back out, to explain that she felt she could not, and yet perversely she heard herself saying calmly, 'Yes, I think so.'

'Good girl.' Doctor Simmonds gave her an avuncular pat. 'I'll take a look at him later this afternoon when I bring the antibiotics.'

When the doctor had gone Lindsay made herself another cup of coffee, stealing herself to go back upstairs and take another look at her patient. What had possessed her to volunteer to look after Lucas?

She *had* volunteered though, and she could hardly back out now. Too late she remembered that she was supposed to be spending the next weekend with Jeremy and his parents. Her heart sank a little. She suspected she was only acceptable to the Byles by virtue of her father's money, and they would not be too pleased at her cancelling the weekend—neither would Jeremy, but surely he would understand that she could hardly desert Lucas? A little reluctantly she went into the study and dialled the number of Jeremy's parents' home. As she had suspected, her explanations as to why she would not be able to stay with them the following weekend met with a frosty reception. 'But surely my dear, someone else could look after your stepbrother . . . Where is his wife? Or surely a nurse could be employed?'

Not wanting to discuss Lucas' divorce with her prospective mother-in-law, Lindsay merely said that Gwen was away, adding that although a nurse could be employed, she felt it almost a duty to stay herself.

It was plain that Irene Byles was not pleased, and for some reason Lindsay found that her displeasure only increased her own determination to stay with Lucas.

'I can't think what Jeremy will have to say,' was her parting comment before she let Lindsay go. 'After all it was his intention to announce your engagement formally next weekend.'

Lindsay always found talking to Jeremy's mother something of a trial. The other woman was an out and out snob, and she maintained an air of condescension toward Lindsay which the latter found particularly trying. Not for the first time a tiny voice urged her to think carefully about committing herself to Jeremy, reminding her that in this case especially to marry the man was to marry the family. Previously she had always managed to convince herself that once they were married Irene's attitude toward her would relax a little, but today she found herself hard to convince. Jeremy's mother resented the fact that she had money, Lindsay knew, even whilst at the same time she wanted that wealth to be brought into the family. She never lost an opportunity to remind Lindsay of the social gap that lay between them, and so far Lindsay had borne her acid barbed remarks with equanimity. Now she found herself wondering if she would be able to mask her resentment when she was actually Jeremy's wife. She even found that she was asking herself why she should have to. Surely as Jeremy's wife she had the right to expect her husband to defend her from his mother's dislike? Disturbed by her own train of thought Lindsay dialled the number of Jeremy's flat and left a brief explanatory message on his answering service. No doubt, as his mother had suggested, Jeremy would not be pleased by her decision to stay with Lucas, but he would be even less pleased to learn that Lucas had not given whole hearted approval to their marriage ... Amazingly, she had been so caught up in her concern for Lucas that she had almost forgotten what had brought her home in the first place, and the rather unkind thought struck her that she had only to say to Jeremy that she was staying with Lucas in the hope of persuading him to change his mind about their engagement and she would undoubtedly have his wholehearted support. Was that really the type of man she wanted to marry, she asked herself wryly; someone who placed money and possessions first in what was important in life? Jeremy had no choice she reminded herself, like her he had been taught almost from birth that certain things were expected of him. It was unfair to blame him for what his parents and upbringing had instilled in him. No one would ever be able to compell Lucas to marry for reasons of expediency, she found herself thinking and then frowned remembering what Doctor Simmonds had said. Surely it couldn't possibly be true that Lucas had married Gwen partially because he was concerned by the gossip about their own relationship? Lindsay could hardly credit it. It seemed so unlike the Lucas she knew . . . the man who had been rendered almost savage with frustration at the loss of his wife. No . . . Doctor Simmonds must have got it wrong.

There was one thing she had to do, Lindsay told herself as she went back upstairs to Lucas, if she was going to stay here and nurse him successfully, and that was that she must put out of her mind completely the events of the previous evening. She must force both her mind and body to forget those moments in Lucas' arms had ever happened; they must be expunged from her memory for all time. He was her stepbrother; she was his sister . . . that was what she must remember . . . not how his skin had felt like hot silk beneath her touch, nor how her body had thrilled with pleasure at his touch upon it, aching for more . . . so much more . . . Stop it, Lindsay cautioned herself, taking a shaky breath. Stop it. Forget all about that—it didn't happen. Forget about it.

Think instead of the practical things, Lindsay

urged herself. If she was going to stay for the
fortnight Doctor Simmonds had said it would take
Lucas to recover, she was going to need more
clothes than those she had brought with her.
Making a mental note to ring Caroline and ask her
to parcel up some things and send them on to her,
Lindsay expelled a faint sigh of relief as she saw
that Lucas was still asleep.

Once again though he had thrown off the
protective bed clothes, and even as she watched he
started to move threshingly his face contorting
into a frown as he muttered incomprehensibly.
'Gwen. . . .' His lips formed his ex-wife's name and
the pain in his voice tormented Lindsay.
Instinctively she went towards him, stroking his
hair back from his fever-hot forehead, murmuring
soothingly to him as she might have done to a
small child, her heart aching in sympathy for him,
even while she knew how much he would hate her
witnessing his weakness. Her touch seemed to
soothe him slightly, and eventually he sank back
into heavy sleep. Lindsay remained where she was
for several minutes, lost in her own thoughts,
wondering painfully why it was that Lucas should
be the one to arouse those feelings inside her she
had once thought herself incapable of experiencing.
She loved him she realised numbingly—not as a
sister . . . not as an adolescent in love with the idea
of love, but as a woman, so deeply and intensely
that for years she had protected herself from the
pain of admitting the truth by denying her feelings
for him. The knowledge hit her like a thunderbolt;
intensely painful, agonisingly real. Too real to be
denied.

She got up and moved restlessly over to the

window, staring blindly out of it. All right, so she loved him? So what? It was an impossible, idiotic love that should be ruthlessly uprooted, she told herself. Lucas certainly did not return her feelings, and even if he had . . .

Even if he had, Lucas was not the man her father would have chosen for her to marry, she acknowledged, and yet her father had loved Lucas like a son. If Lucas had loved her what would she have done, she asked herself, but her senses answered the question for her long before her mind had formed a rational answer. Much as she hated to go against her father's wishes she would have done so. Leaning her elbows on the open window she looked at the distant view, wondering why it should be now, of all times, just when she was on the verge of becoming engaged to someone else that she should discover her real feelings? Could she still marry Jeremy, knowing how she felt about Lucas? If she didn't marry him what was there for her? The pain of loving a man who did not love her in return, the emptiness of a life with no husband or children in it? At least she and Jeremy weren't deceiving one another. They had neither professed to be deeply in love with the other. But when she had agreed to marry Jeremy she hadn't realised how she felt about Lucas, Lindsay reminded herself; she hadn't experienced that fierce starburst of pleasure and need that Lucas had exploded inside her last night. And now that she had? Her thoughts were too muddled for her to analyse them rationally. A sound from the bed alerted her to the reason she was there and she turned towards it.

Lucas had struggled to sit up, pushing aside the

bed clothes in the attempt. He slept in the nude and Lindsay quickly averted her eyes from the lean muscularity of his thighs. He was staring straight at her, his eyes dark and hostile.

'Lindsay? What the the hell are you doing here?'

It seemed impossible after his fever-soaked ramblings, but he was actually lucid and aware of her, his expression telling her that he was anything but pleased with her presence in his room.

'Looking after you,' Lindsay responded tartly, dragging her eyes away from his body. 'You've got a recurrence of your old fever. Doctor Simmonds is coming back to see you later on. He's bringing you some antibiotics.'

'Simmonds is an old woman, there's nothing wrong with me.' His mouth compressed in the hard line Lindsay was familiar with. 'Enjoying playing ministering angel were you? Well sorry as I am to deprive you of the role, there's no . . .' He broke off, his body shuddering violently, sweat springing up in small beads along his chest and forehead. He was shivering so intensely that Lindsay could hear his teeth chattering, and forgetting for a moment his hostility, she hurried over to the bed, dragging the covers up round his body, cautioning him to lie down as she did so.

The way he simply complied and lay back against the pillows, closing his eyes, told her that he was far from well, but remembering what Doctor Simmonds had told her, she picked up the jug of cordial she had brought upstairs and poured out a glass. 'Drink this, Lucas,' she begged him. 'Doctor Simmonds said you were to drink as much as you could ... You're sweating so badly you'll be in danger of dehydrating if you don't.'

He muttered a protest, but struggled to sit up. The effort of moving brought fresh beads of sweat on to his skin, his bones standing out harshly beneath the taut flesh. Instinctively Lindsay made to support him as he drank, sitting down on the side of the bed, so that she could cradle his head. It was obvious that even the small effort of drinking the cordial had exhausted him and Lindsay wasn't surprised when he lapsed back into semi-consciousness, and then sleep.

Once she was sure that he was actually sleeping Lindsay went back downstairs to ring Caroline. After she had expressed her initial surprise at hearing from her flatmate readily agreed to send on some of her clothes.

Tomorrow she would have to ring into work and tell them that she would need to take an extra week's holiday, Lindsay reflected. She would also have to ring Lucas' office and explain to them that he would not be in for some time. She frowned and bit her bottom lip, worrying at it. He would have appointments that would need rescheduling ... but all that could safely be left to Mrs McNaughton who had been her father's secretary and was now Lucas'.

It was six o'clock when Doctor Simmonds finally returned. Lindsay was upstairs with Lucas when she heard the doctor's car. She had been trying to sponge Lucas down, but he had been so restless that her task had been almost impossible. It might have been easier if she had not been so crippled by her own feelings for him, she admitted.

Touching him was a mixture of pain and

pleasure so strong that her muscles ached with the effort of reminding herself that she could only touch him as a sister . . . a nurse.

When she told the doctor about Lucas, brief period of lucidity he nodded his head. 'Yes, it sometimes happens, but don't be deceived by it. It means very little . . . rather like waking up in the middle of the night and holding a conversation with someone—next day you can't remember a thing about it. Are you sure you're going to be able to manage?' he asked her. 'If you want any help?'

'No . . . no, I'll be fine.'

'Well here are the tablets. The instructions are written on the bottle. By tomorrow night you should start to see some improvement . . . His temperature should be down and the sweating less noticeable. I'll call round tomorrow evening though just to check.'

Trying to feed Lucas in his present comatose state would be almost impossible and Doctor Simmonds had told her not to worry about meals. Lucas wasn't going to starve in two days he told her, adding that making sure he had enough to drink was far more important.

She didn't feel particularly hungry herself, but Doctor Simmonds had given Lucas his first tablet, and since he now seemed to be sleeping there was no need to stay with him. She hadn't eaten anything all day, Lindsay reminded herself, but when she was eventually sitting down in front of the omelette she had just cooked her appetite seemed to desert her. Having pushed it half-heartedly around her plate for several minutes she acknowledged that she simply did not want to eat.

There was a television in Lucas' bedroom, and she could go up there and watch it, keeping an eye on her patient at the same time, but first she would have a shower. She felt sticky and tired, worn out as much by her own emotions as by her physical exertions in lifting and sponging the heavy maleness of Lucas' body.

CHAPTER FIVE

FEELING slightly refreshed by her shower Lindsay pulled on an old cotton towelling robe she had found at the back of her wardrobe. She remembered it from her teens and guessed that she must have left it behind when she moved out. The towelling was well worn and comfortable, and although the garment was more practical than glamorous, Lindsay felt more comfortable in it than she had done in her cashmere skirt and sweater.

Jeremy would have a fit if he could see her now, she thought ruefully, surveying her shiny, make-up free face and heavy swathe of hair. Jeremy liked her to look elegant and soignée, slightly cool and remote. Well she looked anything but that now, she thought, studying her own reflection briefly. With her hair down and no make-up on she didn't look very much different from the teenager who had stared in this same mirror six years ago. Tying the sash of the robe she got up and went downstairs to the kitchen. Sheila, she remembered used to make a fruit drink that Lucas had been particularly fond of. Perhaps if she could make some of it, she might be able to coax him to drink a little more. She thought she could remember most of the ingredients, and luckily she found all the fruit she needed in the cool larder, just off the kitchen.

When she had made up the drink Lindsay put it in

a large flask in the fridge. Once it was chilled she could take it upstairs with her. She had looked in on Lucas before she came down and he had still been deeply, if somewhat restlessly, asleep. Soon it would be time to give him another tablet, and with a bit of luck she would be able to do so without waking him up. Sleep was the best medicine he could have Doctor Simmonds had told her, but he had also gone on to say that his present half-unconscious state was more of a fever induced coma than natural sleep. It wasn't dangerous the doctor had hastily assured Lindsay when he saw her expression, but neither was it particularly beneficial. She should be prepared for further bouts of feverish rambling as the illness ran its course, and also the fact that once he was well again Lucas would probably have little recollection of his illness.

Lindsay was just on her way upstairs with the chilled drink when the phone rang in the study. She picked up the receiver, automatically giving the number.

'Lindsay is that you?'

Jeremy sounded terse and angry.

'I take it you got my message.'

'Yes, but not before mother had rung me to complain about you cancelling next weekend. Lindsay, what the devil's going on?'

'I told your mother, Lucas is ill . . .'

'Yes, so she told me, but I can't see why that necessitates you staying on there. He has a wife doesn't he? And God knows with all his money he should be able to pay for a nurse if that's what's needed. I want you to come back to London, Lindsay,' Jeremy continued. 'I can understand your concern—after all he is your brother, but you can't just drop everything to look after him. Where's his wife?'

'Er . . . Gwen's . . . away at the moment.' Why on earth hadn't she told Jeremy the truth, Lindsay asked herself ruefully, as she listened to his further objections. Not for any sinister reason, simply because she couldn't cope with the further complications explaining would involve. Jeremy always liked to have all his 'i's' dotted and his 't's' crossed, and she simply didn't have the energy right now to explain to him that Gwendolin and Lucas were divorced.

'Gwen isn't here, Jeremy, and I feel I ought to stay. Mrs James, Lucas' housekeeper is nursing her sick sister, and Lucas is alone in the house. He could employ a nurse of course, but I feel that I should stay.'

Don't ask me any more questions Jeremy, she pleaded mentally. I just can't cope with them at the moment. The truth was, if she could bring herself to face it, that she simply preferred to stay here with Lucas than return to London and Jeremy. Of course it was not quite as simple as that. Lucas was ill, and she knew she wouldn't have a moment's peace if she left him in someone else's care.

'Well yes, I can understand that . . . but I do think you might have made alternative arrangements for this weekend. Surely someone else could have stayed with him then. After all, it was supposed to be our engagement party.'

He sounded aggrieved and possibly with good cause, Lindsay acknowledged fair-mindedly, but when Jeremy was annoyed he was inclined to sulk and she didn't feel she could cope with soothing him right now. And besides ... She took a deep breath. 'Yes ... Jeremy about our engagement ...' She paused half of her horrified by what she was doing, the other half egging her on.

'Yes?'

'I'm ... I'm beginning to wonder if it would be such a good idea after all ... I ...'

Jeremy made a small explosive sound of anger, and Lindsay could picture him frowning into the receiver. 'Lindsay, I don't understand what's got into you,' he complained angrily. 'You're acting completely out of character. First you upset mother by backing out of next weekend; then you start saying you've got doubts about our engagement. What you need, my girl, is a holiday.'

'Jeremy ...'

'We'll talk about it when you get back,' he told her stiffly, adding, 'I thought you were a sensible woman, Lindsay. Indeed that was one of the things about you that most appealed to me.'

'Was it? Strange, I thought it was my money.' Lindsay was appalled to hear herself saying the words, her voice dry and unfamiliar. That Jeremy too was shocked by her comment was obvious from the tense sound of his breathing.

'Lindsay, you're obviously not yourself. I don't know what's got into you, but it isn't something we can discuss over the telephone. We'll discuss it when you return to London.' He hung up before she could make any comment, hardly surprisingly really, Lindsay thought wryly. Poor Jeremy, she had been extremely unfair and unkind to him. After all it was hardly his fault that she had discovered she was in love with Lucas.

Still frowning she went upstairs and walked irresolutely into Lucas' bedroom, standing by the door while she studied him. Even in sleep the aura of power emanating from him was extraordinarily strong. Always at the back of her mind although she had hidden the knowledge from herself she had been aware of his masculinity; of the strong pull he exercised over her senses. It had been there when she was a teenager, but her malleable adolescent emotions had been unable to cope with the intensity of that magnetism and instead of admitting her love for him she had subtly altered it, making it more acceptable, taming it ... but there was an elemental wildness about Lucas that refused to be tamed. Just for a moment a pagan image of him as a lover flashed across her mind, and a low, raw sound of pain broke from her throat as she pictured him sharing this bed with Gwendolin. Her body trembled convulsively as though it felt his touch, and Lindsay backed nervily further out of the door. What was happening to her? Far too many years of repressed emotions and denied feelings were catching up on her, that was what was happening and she didn't know if she could cope with it. Her body ached and throbbed with a tense nervy urgency that made her restless and afraid. But afraid of what? That Lucas was going to get off the bed and seduce her? Hardly likely; either that he would, or if he did that she would be afraid ... No what she was afraid of was the violence of her own responses to the mental suggestion; the fierce coursing need that destroyed all her pre-conceived ideas of herself. Sexually cold ... withdrawn, remote; that was how others saw her and how she was used to seeing herself, but suddenly that false image had cracked and she was finding it difficult to come to terms with the truth. She thought of the stream of girls who had passed through Lucas' life before he met and married Gwendolin; she had always found something in them to dislike, and Lucas, she remembered had been lazily amused by her criticisms. She frowned again. Surely a man with his experience must have realised what lay at the root of it. Had he known? Had he guessed what she had kept secret from herself? The thought made her squirm uncomfortably. It was one thing to acknowledge to herself that she loved and physically desired him to an extent that was still new enough to rock her off her heels, but to be forced to come to terms with the possibility that Lucas himself knew as well and probably had known for years, was something else. Now that she had time to think about her reactions her own naïvety amazed her. How often had she wanted to touch him, only to draw back instinctively . . . how often had she been close to weeping for the gap that yawned between them, aching for the days when they had been close?

But Lucas did not feel about her the way she felt about him, and never would she must accept that. As she watched him he stirred restlessly and she forced herself to approach the bed. It was time for him to have a drink and his tablet. Willing her mind to empty itself of the tormenting memory of imagining him as her lover Lindsay applied herself to her task. She was just congratulating herself on doing so successfully when his fingers fastened round her wrist, his eyes opening wide to stare into hers.

'Lindsay.'

She started to pull away automatically but he wouldn't let her go. Even gripped by fever he was still far stronger than her, and she knew that tomorrow the fragile bones of her wrist would bear bruise marks from his fingers.

'Stay here with me. Don't go.' His eyes were still fastened on hers but they had lost their sharp alertness, and were smokey with pain and exhaustion. He was rambling again Lindsay guessed, probably not even wholly aware of who he was holding.

Sanity demanded that she pull away, but the need to comfort and soothe him was too powerful. With her free hand she stroked his forehead, smoothing away his frown. His skin was hot and moist, but no longer burning as it had done earlier. Under the soft stroke of his fingers, his frown relaxed, his eyes slowly closing. Almost without realising what she was doing, Lindsay pushed his hair back off his forehead. It felt like silk beneath her fingertips, so dark and heavy, unlike her own. This need to explore the textures of another person's body was unknown to her, but already frighteningly addictive. She wanted to touch him and to go on touching. To explore the hard muscles lying beneath his skin, to know the reality of him in the most intimate and personal sense of the word. Longing racked her in sharp, violent pangs, emotions she had hitherto never imagined existing making her slender frame shudder uncontrollably. She knew she should stop what she was doing; it was after all gross violation of Lucas' privacy; an intimacy he would not have granted her had he been in full possession of his

senses, but alongside her deep sense of inner shame
was a hunger she simply could not control. And he
was responding to her touch, relaxing under it, his
fierce grip of her wrist lessening slightly as she
stroked her fingers through his hair, exploring the
hard bones of his skull, aching with a reckless need
to communicate to him how she felt; to pour out
her love for him; to abandon herself completely
and no longer be Lindsay Ferris but instead part
of one unit that was comprised both of herself and
Lucas.

The direction her thoughts were taking hit her
like a douche of icy water, reality forcing her to
stop what she was doing and to drag her eyes
away from the exposed nudity of his upper body.

For God's sake, she chided herself bitterly.
What's the matter with you? You're behaving like
a comic strip frustrated spinster overcome with
lust at the sight of a male body. A half hysterical
burst of laughter escaped her. Dear God . . . what
was happening to her? Gently she tugged away
from Lucas' grasp, but to her consternation
instead of letting her go his grip tightened again,
and he muttered something in his sleep, turning
towards her. As he moved the sheet slipped further
down his body, exposing the hard line of his thigh.
His skin was tanned and sleek, and she found
herself wondering where he had got that all over
bronzing and with whom? Not with Gwendolin
apparently. A dart of agony pierced through her as
she was forced to contemplate the reality of Lucas
as some other woman's lover. And he would be an
expert; she knew that instinctively . . . a master of
sensual expertise, giving pleasure as well as taking
it. Her skin burned but she still shivered,

automatically reaching down to pull the covers
over him with her free hand.

Almost instantly it was grasped and made a
prisoner like its twin. Smothering her verbal
protest, Lindsay tried to tug free. Lucas had no
knowledge of what he was doing. His eyes were
still closed, his forehead creased in a new frown,
which deepened with every attempt she made to
break away. Without opening his eyes he muttered
thickly. 'No . . . no . . . don't leave me,' and the
raw need in his voice pierced her with pain. Who
did he think he was holding? Gwendolin? The wife
who had left him and whom he obviously loved far
more than she had ever imagined, but then she
seemed to have an acute facility for self-deceit, and
perhaps she had not seen the real depth of his
feelings for his wife, because she had not wanted
to? She braced herself on the edge of the bed with
one knee, trying to lever herself free without
waking him up. She had no doubt that she was the
last woman Lucas would want to find in his arms,
but as she balanced herself precariously on the
bed, his grip on her wrists suddenly tightened and
Lindsay looked down to find him watching her
with smokily hazed eyes. He made a sound in his
throat and pulled her down beside him on to the
bed, his hands freeing her wrists, one arm holding
her against the mattress . . .

'Lucas . . . it's me Lindsay,' she protested
huskily. 'Let me get up.' She was wasting her
breath. His eyes had closed again and his skin was
flushed, the incoherent mutterings he was making
confirming her suspicion that he had lapsed back
into his fever. Doctor Simmonds had warned her
that it could happen, but how was she going to get

free, she wondered wryly. Lucas had wrapped one arm completely round her, and even as she struggled, he rolled over, flinging one powerful leg over hers, half lying on top of her, his weight pinning her to the bed, making it impossible for her to move at all. She tried to wake him, shaking him quickly, but it was no use. When her fingers brushed his skin it felt burning hot again, and she knew that he was completely unaware of what he had done.

Sighing faintly Lindsay thought wryly that it was just her luck to end up in bed with the man she loved while he remained completely oblivious to her presence.

She didn't mean to fall asleep; but the day had been a particularly exhausting one, and at first when something wakened her, she wasn't even sure where she was. It took her name, muttered by Lucas, in a questioning slurred voice, to recall her to reality, freezing her within the circle of his arms, her senses immediately aware of their intimacy; of Lucas' body half lying over hers, of the pressure of his forearm just below her breasts, his breathing erratic and audible close to her ear.

She held her breath automatically, as she waited for him to demand to know what she was doing in his bed, her eyes fearful and defensive as she forced herself to look into his. In the half light of the lamp lit room, his eyes gleamed dove grey rather than the cold metallic hardness she was more used to. 'Lindsay?' There was still a question in his voice, but the question was a different one, the sensual enquiry in the husky way he said her name, underlined by the slow drift of his fingers along her arm.

'Lucas!' He obviously had no idea what he was doing ... He was in the grip of a fever, Lindsay reminded herself desperately, trying to push away from him, as she fought against the slow, languorous pleasure flooding through her veins at his touch. 'Lucas, let me go,' she begged tensely. 'Lucas, it's me, Lindsay.'

Her protest was silenced by the questing warmth of his mouth as it found her lips. Found and explored them with a slow sensuality that totally destroyed her defences. Her lips when Lucas finally released them felt soft and swollen, and Lindsay ran a nervous tongue over their contours, the movement arrested as she caught the hoarse, thick sound Lucas stifled in his throat.

'Let me do that for you.'

This couldn't be happening Lindsay thought crazily, feeling her body melt into aching compliance at the slow drift of his tongue against her parted lips.

Lucas couldn't possibly know what he was doing. But she did ... she was not in the grip of a mind-distorting fever ... she was not weakened by illness and drugs. She must ...

Whatever it was she must do was forgotten as Lucas bit softly against her mouth, exploring its feminine contours, just as his hands were exploring her body. She was melting ... on fire ... aching with the delirious pleasure of his touch ... no longer Lindsay Ferris but some formless mindless creature created only to meet and match his need.

His eyes closed, Lucas muttered thick, husky sounds of pleasure against her skin, inciting her to respond to him, to touch him as he was touching her. His skin felt hot and moist beneath her shaking fingers, but when she tried to withdraw them, he captured her wrist, and unfurled her tightly closed fingers, placing her hand palm down against his heart.

'Feel what you do to me.'

She could feel his heart racing against her hand, its beat fast and unsteady, unconsciously she smoothed her fingers over his skin and was shaken by the hoarse sound of pleasure he made against her throat. What was happening to her? She was drowning in a vast sea of sensual delight drowning without making any attempt to save herself; without *wanting* to save herself, totally seduced by the magic wrought by touch by the lure of Lucas' maleness and what it did to all her senses. It was like suddenly coming alive; like being blind and suddenly able to see; deaf and able to hear ... the full weight of so much hitherto unknown pleasure crashed down over her, and unknowingly she sobbed Lucas' name, her hands clutching wildly at his shoulders as his lips caressed her throat, exploring the long, tense arch of it, seducing her away from reason and reality. She heard someone moan and realised it was herself. The tip of Lucas' tongue explored the convolutions of her ear, tracing them, teasing and tormenting her until she could endure it no longer and she was moaning his name, in a hoarse unfamiliar little voice, her pulses thudding out a wild cacophony of primaeval pleasure. It was all too much too soon, like being engulfed in all the pleasures of the senses at once, and yet in some ways it was almost too much to bear.

Lucas was touching her bare skin now, pushing aside the lapels of her robe. The sash had worked loose, and Lindsay wasn't sure whether pleasure or anguish was uppermost; which was the more powerful feeling bursting into life inside her when Lucas touched her breasts, his hands enclosing them, possessing and yet somehow subtly conveying to her by his touch that to possess was to be seduced by the femininity of her.

Lindsay was aware of her nipples hardening; aching; and as though she were somehow standing outside herself, watching she saw the wanton arch of her body, enticing and encouraging Lucas to pull her robe completely free of her body; to study its feminine contours and to marvel at the subtle play of light and colour against her pale skin.

'Lindsay . . . My God . . .'

His voice was a muffled whisper of pain and longing, the delicate, almost tentative touch of his tongue painting aching circles round her nipples banishing all the urgings of caution and common sense. So what if he doesn't really know what he's doing, a reckless inner voice whispered softly. *You* know . . . you will always have the memory of this no matter what comes after. The memory and the anguish, not to mention the pain and self-contempt, common sense warned her, but she was long, long past listening to common sense, long, long past doing anything other than weaving her fingers into Lucas' hair and clasping him against her body when his mouth opened over her nipple exploring its sensitivity with delicate precision that bordered on torment, until Lindsay discovered that one way of relieving the sensations he was arousing inside her was to touch her burning lips to his skin; to let her fingers explore the alien maleness of his body.

Fire fed on fire, she reminded herself hazily as she recorded his body's response to her touch; felt it, in the increasing passionate demand of his mouth against her skin. Tasting, exploring, inciting . . . wanting . . . And he *did* want her. She could feel his wanting in his touch; in the hard aroused pressure of his body against her own. Deep down in the pit of her stomach she ached for him with a savagery that half shocked her. There was nothing she wanted more right at this moment than his total possession; than the satisfaction of knowing he wanted her to the point where that wanting obliterated everything else, including his self-control. But how could a man who didn't really know what he was doing exhibit self-control. Pain and self-disgust ripped through her body. Dear God what was she thinking of? What madness was possessing her? Lucas had no idea who he held in his arms. She could have been anybody . . . literally. Nausea flooded through her stomach and she tensed against it, hating herself almost as much as she hated the cold little voice inside her forcing her to realise the truth. Why now, her senses pleaded . . . why not later . . . after . . .

After what? After Lucas had possessed her? Because that's *all* it would be, a physical appeasement of a physical need . . . nothing else . . . But she had needs too . . .

Merely physical ones; that same inner voice demanded to know. No, of course not. If that was the case she would have taken a lover years ago. And she was deceiving herself if she thought Lucas actually cared for her. He did not. His hand was on her thigh, but suddenly she felt cold and empty, all desire gone and an acute sense of self loathing taking its place. She moved away from him and miraculously Lucas released her. 'Gwen?' There was an uncertainty in his voice that confirmed all she had been telling herself, and it tore her apart to know that he probably thought he had been caressing his ex-wife; if indeed he was aware of touching her at all. Just at that moment he opened his eyes and looked straight into hers, and Lindsay knew with a fatal sick certainty that he knew exactly who she was; that right now he was completely lucid and free of fever. Even the way he said her name, smokily with bitter anger, held a familiar ring to it. His eyes left her face and his glance raked down along her body, and Lindsay was sickly aware of her provocatively bared breasts; the nipples still tautly aroused. The contempt in Lucas' eyes when they finally locked on hers once again was more than she could bear. She hid her face in her hands with a stifled moan, but he prised her fingers away, forcing her to look back at him as he gripped her jaw.

'What's the matter, Lindsay? Are you ashamed of wanting me? Of wanting *sex*?'

The way he said it made it sound sordid, so much so that Lindsay felt herself shrivel with pain and humiliation. What could she say to him? How could she explain away the totally unexplainable? Her very presence in his bed . . . in his arms said it all.

'I wonder what your precious Jeremy would have to say about this? Two days away from him and . . .' he reached for her, as unable to endure any more, Lindsay tore herself away from him and off the bed, but she managed to evade him,

Say yes to free gifts worth $17.75

Say YES to a rendezvous with romance and you'll get 4 classic love stories—FREE! You'll get an LCD digital quartz watch—FREE! You'll get a stylish ballpoint pen—FREE! And you'll get a delightful surprise—FREE! These gifts carry a total value of $17.75—but you can have them without spending even a penny!

MONEY-SAVING HOME DELIVERY!

Say YES to Harlequin's Home Reader Service and you'll enjoy the convenience of previewing brand-new books every month, delivered right to your home before they appear in stores. Each book is yours for only $1.75—20¢ less than the retail price.

SPECIAL EXTRAS—FREE!

You'll also get our monthly newsletter, packed with news of your favorite authors and upcoming books—FREE! Four times a year, you'll receive our members' magazine *Romance Digest*—FREE! And you'll periodically receive our special-edition *Harlequin Bestsellers* to preview for 10 days—FREE!

Say yes to a Harlequin love affair. Complete, detach and mail your Free Offer Card today!

Harlequin HOME READER SERVICE

✲ FREE OFFER CARD ✲

4 FREE BOOKS   **FREE PEN**

Place YES
sticker here

FREE WATCH   **FREE SURPRISE**

Please send me my 4 Harlequin Presents novels, free, along with my free watch, pen and surprise gift. Then send me 8 books every month, as they come off the presses, and bill me just $1.75 per book (20¢ less than retail), with no extra charges for shipping and handling. If I am not completely satisfied, I may return a shipment and cancel at any time. *The free books and gifts remain mine to keep!* 108 CIP CAJ9

Name_____
(PLEASE PRINT)

Address_____Apt_____

City_____

Prov/State_____Postal Code/Zip_____

FREE—*digital watch and matching pen*

You'll love your new LCD quartz digital watch with its
genuine leather strap. And the slim matching pen is
perfect for writing that special person. Both are yours
FREE as our gift of love.

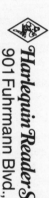

sobbing in agonising breaths of air from a throat too tight to enable her to breathe properly as she dragged her robe back on. Her fingers were shaking so much she couldn't tie the belt. She couldn't bear to look at Lucas. 'What would daddy have said?' Lucas mocked . . . 'Is that the only way you can enjoy sex, Lindsay? By stealing satisfaction from a man who doesn't know what he's doing?'

The pain was more than she could endure. Without being able to respond to him Lindsay left the room, praying that he would not come after her. How could she have behaved like that she demanded of herself half an hour later, standing under the chilly lash of her own shower, scrubbing her flesh as though she wanted to mortify it. How could she have done it . . . She shuddered and trembled remembering the feelings Lucas had aroused inside her. Feelings that if she was truthful, were even now, still there.

No, no . . . her aching throat screamed the denial defiantly, but there was no one to her hear above the lash of the water. No one to see the tears that streamed down her face to mingle with the icy spray. Tomorrow morning she would have to leave. She would have to find Lucas a nurse. She couldn't stay now . . . She could not!

CHAPTER SIX

LINDSAY would have given anything not to have had to face Lucas the next morning, but her pride would not allow her to simply leave without seeing him. She twisted her hair into an elegant knot on top of her head and applied her make-up with more than usual care, hoping to hide the fact that her skin was too pale, and her eyes still sore from all the bitter tears she had cried. She dressed with care too, a slim pleated skirt and a toning buttoned up to the neck blouse. The sort of clothes Jeremy liked to see her wearing.

She was downstairs in the kitchen when the postman knocked and handed her a large parcel. Caroline had been as good as her word and had sent her some more clothes. Well she wouldn't be needing those now, she told herself as she prepared a tray for Lucas, her stomach muscles tensing as she tried to come to terms with the reality of what had happened. Even now while her mind scorned and lashed her for her weakness, her body still ached betrayingly, still wanted him, she acknowledged numbly.

Outside his bedroom door she hesitated, not wanting to go in but knowing she must. He stirred as she walked in, opening his eyes to look at her. Just for a moment she thought she saw intense pleasure softening their harsh grey, but she knew she had been imagining things when he demanded harshly, 'Lindsay, what are you doing here?'

Lindsay trembled, wishing now that she had simply left without seeing him, but she hadn't been able to do that. She had needed to assure herself that he was all right. 'Still hoping to persuade me to change my mind and sanction your marriage is that it?' As he taunted her, he thrust aside the bed clothes, ignoring her half stifled protest. He was half-way out of bed when he sank back against the mattress, his skin grey and stretched tautly over his bones. 'God, I feel as weak as a kitten,' he muttered, shakenly. 'What the devil . . .'

'You've been ill,' Lindsay reminded him, curbing the urge to go over to him and smooth the tangled hair back from his forehead. Comfort from her was the last thing he would want.

'Ill?' He stared at her, so obviously nonplussed and disbelieving that it was obvious that he wasn't aware of the return of his fever.

'Yes,' Lindsay explained patiently. 'You've had a bout of fever . . . don't you remember?'

Her heart was in her mouth as she looked at him. Could it be possible that for once the Gods were going to smile on her and Lucas genuinely could not remember anything about last night? She knew that Doctor Simmonds had pointed out the possibility of him not being able to remember anything that had happened while he was semi-delirious, but last night he had seemed so normal . . .

'All I can remember is you storming out saying you were going back to London, after I'd refused to sanction your marriage,' Lucas told her grimly. 'Now you're telling me that I've been ill.'

'So ill that I had to send for Doctor Simmonds,' Lindsay assured him, picking up the medication from the table next to the bed. 'You've been delirious and practically only half conscious for nearly forty-eight hours Lucas, and Doctor Simmons told me it could be a fortnight before you're properly back on your feet again.'

'Forty-eight hours?' He sat up frowning heavily, unaware apparently that the sheet had slipped downwards revealing the taut muscles of his stomach. It took a considerable effort for Lindsay to drag her eyes away, and she knew that her pulses were racing uncomfortably, her body traitorously reminding her of last night and things she had promised herself she was going to forget. 'Damnation ... That means that today's Tuesday, and Don Carter, one of our American customers is flying in today. He wants to talk business with me, and I'd invited him to stay here. Hell ... we need that contract too. Where's the 'phone, I'll have to try and get him booked in somewhere. I suppose Mrs James isn't back yet?'

When Lindsay shook her head, he swore briefly again, his glance suddenly sharpening as it fell on her. 'Dare I ask if you would stay on here for a couple of days to act as my hostess?' He said it quite casually and yet Lindsay had the distinct impression that beneath his surface coolness, he was tense. Was the American's contract so important to him that he was prepared to risk her refusal ... that he was actually prepared to ask her to help him? Pain and anguish smote her. Dear God, didn't he realise that there wasn't anything she would not do for him?

Her common sense warned her that she ought to refuse; that to stay was to lay herself open to more pain, and yet the temptation to stay ... to be with him was too great for her to withstand.

'I'd already arranged to stay here anyway,' she told him as nonchalantly as she could. So . . .'

'You had?' He frowned again, 'Why? On Sunday you were all set to leave. Hoping to persuade me to change my mind were you?'

His cynicism appalled and hurt her, and her temper, never very controllable when she was around him, exploded painfully inside her. 'You would think that,' she said bitterly, 'I don't suppose it's occurred to you that I was worried about you . . . That I might have decided to stay because you were ill, that . . .'

'That what? You thought you might be able to use my weakness to coax me into having a change of heart?' He laughed derisively. 'No way, Lindsay. Why the sudden urgent desire to marry anyway?' he demanded, 'You're not carrying his child are you?'

Lindsay couldn't keep the shocked expression off her face. 'Oh come on, Lindsay,' Lucas jeered. 'I wasn't born yesterday. You live a pretty freewheeling life in London, at least according to what Gwen told me. You and your precious Jeremy must be lovers, and given that it's not impossible that you might be carrying his child. However, since you're obviously not—and don't want to be, if your present expression is anything to go by— you'd better take care that you don't become pregnant. I doubt he'll marry you once he discovers that marriage to you doesn't come with the guarantee of your father's wealth.'

'You . . . you bastard!' Lindsay flung at him fiercely, 'For your information, I . . .'

'Yes,' he drawled mockingly, 'You . . .'

I haven't had any lover, she had been about to

say, and Lindsay could only stare at him in
appalled confusion, horrified by what she had
been about to admit to him. It seemed impossible
that he couldn't remember anything of the previous
night, but it was obvious that this was the case—
she ought to be thanking her lucky stars for that
... not arguing with him about her marriage to
Jeremy, she told herself, adding the mental rider
that if she had any sense at all, she wouldn't be
here at all, but on her way back to London.

'You don't want his child, is that what you were
going to say? But he'll expect you to produce a son
and heir for him, Lindsay, otherwise who's going
to benefit from all your father's money. How does
it feel to be wanted for your father's wealth or are
you still trying to pretend to yourself that it's you
he wants . . .'

'Would that be so impossible?' Lindsay seethed,
hurt beyond caution by his cruel taunts. 'Am I so
undesirable, Lucas?'

'Are you asking me that as a stepbrother or as a
man, Lindsay?'

She couldn't bear to look at him in case he saw
how she felt in her eyes, but he obviously
misunderstood her silence because he laughed
harshly and mocked. 'Hating me as you do
Lindsay, I'm surprised you didn't simply leave me
to my fate. Who knows my fever might have
proved fatal and then you'd have no problems
would you?'

Gritting her teeth Lindsay responded curtly,
'Obviously I'm not as callous as you are Lucas.
Here's your breakfast.' She thrust the tray towards
him, and saw him pull a wry face over the juice
and coffee she had brought him.

'Nothing to eat? What are you trying to do? Starve me?'

'Have you ever tried to feed a semi-conscious man?' Lindsay responded. 'If you want something to eat, I'll go and make it for you—after I've got a room ready for your guest. When is he expected by the way?'

'Lunch time, and yes I would like something to eat, but I'll get up for it. Lying here in bed with you glowering at me like that gives me the most insecure feeling ... I don't understand why ... probably something to do with the fact that every time I turn my back on you I'm half expecting you to stab a knife in it.'

The bitter mockery in his eyes as he studied her made her want to cry. Why ... why was he like this with her. All right he couldn't, didn't love her as she loved him ... he was hurting over Gwendolin as well, but once they had been good friends and companions; once he had treated her with affection.

'Give it up, Lindsay,' he drawled tightly, 'Playing the ministering angel won't make me change my mind.'

The temptation to slam down the tray and tell him she was leaving was overwhelming, but Lindsay knew she could not do it. She *wanted* to stay that was why ... she knew that by doing so all she was doing was laying up more pain and hurt for herself, but she was like an addict hooked on a drug which she knew was destroying her, powerless to free herself from her addiction. But instead of telling him she was leaving all she could manage was a tightly angry, 'Lucas I don't need your consent to marry Jeremy, and don't forget I

can always appeal to my father's solicitor if I think
you're being unreasonable.'

She didn't wait for his response, half running
out of his room and slamming the door behind
her. At the top of the stairs, she paused to breathe
deeply and steady herself. She was crazy to let him
get to her like this. By rights by now she should be
on her way back to London. She tried to imagine
his reaction if she were to walk back into his room
and calmly announce that last night they had been
on the verge of becoming lovers. He wouldn't
believe her of course. Smothering a bitter laugh
she went into the kitchen. If they were to have a
guest, she had better check there was enough food
in the house to feed him.

She need not have worried. Mrs James was an
admirable housekeeper. Both the cupboards and
the freezer were well stocked, and Lindsay knew
from past experience that the shop in the village
could be relied upon to deliver at short notice if
she rang them up with an order.

She had just finished preparing a light breakfast
for Lucas—scrambled eggs on toast which she
remembered had always been one of his favourites,
when Doctor Simmonds arrived. They went
upstairs together, and found Lucas on the point of
getting up.

'Oh no, you don't,' Doctor Simmonds told him
jovially. 'You're a long way from leaving that bed
yet my boy.'

Lindsay repressed a grin at hearing Lucas thus
addressed, but she hadn't been quite quick enough
to hide it from him, and he retaliated by saying
softly, 'I think you'd better leave, Lindsay, before
I prove Doctor Simmonds wrong by getting out of

this bed. I sleep in the raw and I don't want to offend any maidenly sensibilities.'

To Lindsay's relief Doctor Simmonds laughed. 'You won't get away with it that way, Lucas,' he told his patient, 'and as for shocking Lindsay,' he shook his head, calmly pushing a thermometer into Lucas' mouth before he could protest, 'After spending the last couple of days listening to your ravings, and sponging you down every two hours, I suspect she's probably shock proof, isn't that right Lindsay?'

She managed a brief shrug, too stunned by the expression in Lucas' eyes as he stared at her to do anything more. Doctor Simmonds removed the thermometer, and Lucas quickly masked his eyes with the heavy thickness of his lashes. When he raised them again, the hot, bitter anger that had been in his eyes was gone, his expression coolly bland.

'I regret to say I can't remember a thing about it. I hope I didn't give you too much trouble.' His eyes said that he hoped he had, but Lindsay ignored them. Her heart was thudding in terrible agitation.

'Doctor Simmonds said you probably wouldn't remember much about what happened while you were delirious,' she said briefly, not daring to look at Lucas, in case he saw the fear in her eyes.

'That's right,' the doctor agreed. 'I warned her not to take too much notice of any brief periods of lucidity you might have, but the fever's broken properly now.'

'And I can get up?' Lucas enquired with assumed meekness.

'Not until this afternoon at the earliest.' Doctor

Simmonds turned to Lindsay. 'Don't bother to see me out my dear, I can find my own way. I dare say you're going to have your hands full for the next few days. He won't make an easy patient.'

Lindsay would have followed him to the now closed door, but Lucas stopped her by grabbing hold of her wrist. The bruises he had inflicted the previous night were painful, her skin discoloured. When she flinched away from him he frowned down at them, and Lindsay could see him almost measuring the betraying marks with his fingers.

'I see I did give you some trouble,' he said quietly at last. Too quietly Lindsay thought praying that he wasn't going to remember what had happened.

'Not much,' she lied quickly. 'Apart from confusing me with Gwen once or twice.' There, that should throw him off the track if he was in danger of remembering. Let him think if he did that she had believed he was confusing her with his ex-wife.

'Really? How very odd of me.' He was frowning at her, studying her almost as though he could see into her brain and read the truth there, Lindsay reflected. Her wrist still lay encircled by his fingers but she dared not pull away; she dared not do anything other than simply stand there willing her breathing to slow and her heart to stop jumping so painfully.

'Was that how you got these?' He raised her wrist indicating her bruises.

Lindsay managed a casual shrug.

'Tell me more about these periods of lucidity,' Lucas drawled, 'I'm beginning to get very curious about them?'

Lindsay's heart thumped. She felt as though she were on the brink of a very deep chasm. One false movement . . . one careless word and she would be plunging down into it.

'Oh they were nothing,' she lied trying to laugh it off.

'Nothing?' Lucas studied her bruises with a faintly brooding air. 'You call these nothing?'

'You didn't know what you were doing,' Lindsay told him. 'Like I said you . . . you confused me with Gwen . . . You didn't want me to leave.'

He had been studying her wrist almost dispassionately, but as she said these last words, his head came up, his eyes fastening on hers. His silent, intense scrutiny was unnerving, and Lindsay felt herself starting to tremble, as much from that as from the sensation of his fingers curled round her wrist.

'Are you trying to tell me that I wanted you to stay here with me because I thought you were my wife?'

Why was she feeling so nervous? There was nothing untoward in that.

Taking a deep breath Lindsay said shakily, 'Yes, I . . . You . . . were very feverish.'

The 'phone rang shrilly, releasing Lindsay from the tension gripping her. Lucas released her wrist to pick up the receiver, and taking a shaky breath Lindsay retreated towards the door. She would have left him if Lucas hadn't frowned and shaken his head, indicating that he wanted her to stay. His conversation was brief and faintly terse and listening to it, Lindsay realised that he was talking to his secretary.

'Yes. I've just realised about that, but it's all right. Lindsay is going to stay on here and act as my hostess. We'd already arranged for a car to pick him up at the airport hadn't we, and I've got most of the papers I'll need here. I brought them home this weekend to study. No . . . don't worry about it, if there are any problems I'll be in touch.'

When he replaced the receiver, he was frowning slightly. 'I need some papers from downstairs, could you bring them up for me please, Lindsay.'

It was obvious that he was no longer interested in talking about his illness and with a sigh of relief Lindsay nodded her head, listening to him while he explained what he wanted.

It was just after three o'clock when she heard a car pulling up outside, and subduing a nervous feathering in her stomach she hurried to the front door, guessing that it would be their American visitor.

He was nothing like she had visualised, being short and plump, rather like a jolly little Father Christmas, with his white hair and ruddy complexion, surely far too good-natured and roly-poly to be a hardened entrepreneur, which was what Lucas had assured her he was.

He greeted her warmly, paying off his taxi and staring round admiringly. 'Say this is a mighty fine place you've got here Mrs Armitage, he commented, turning to admire the view.

Mrs Armitage. Lindsay gulped. Obviously he didn't know about Lucas' divorce and had mistaken her for Gwen. Not wanting to embarrass him by correcting him in front of the taxi driver, she made a mental note to tell Lucas about his mistake, turning to lead the way into the house.

She had been out into the garden to cut some fresh flowers and they made a bold splash of colour in the hall. He stopped to admire them, beaming at Lindsay. 'My late wife, God bless her, used to love freshly cut flowers. Us men tend not to bother with those feminine touches when we live alone.'

'I'll show you up to your room,' Lindsay offered. 'You must be tired after such a long flight.'

'You're right, although I do cross the Atlantic pretty frequently. Lucas . . .'

'I'm afraid he's in bed at the moment,' Lindsay explained forestalling his question. 'Nothing serious, just a bout of a recurring fever he suffers from. Something he picked up in Africa when he was a boy. Fortunately he's over the worst now and he'll be getting up for dinner this evening.' She smiled ruefully as she stopped by the guest suite door.

'I guess he won't make the easiest of patients,' Don Carter agreed with a hearty laugh. 'But you should have let me know. I could have postponed my visit.'

'Say, this is a real fine room,' he exclaimed as Lindsay ushered him into the guest suite.'

Gwen's interior decorators had done well with this suite, retaining its traditional atmosphere. The bedroom and its adjoining sitting room overlooked the gardens, and Lindsay had put flowers in here too, plus a selection of magazines and a tin of biscuits she had found downstairs in the cupboard.

'Please come downstairs whenever you feel ready,' Lindsay invited. 'We won't be having dinner until eight, but I thought you might care for a snack before then. I'll just go and tell Lucas that you've arrived,' she added, turning back to the door, and heading for Lucas' room.

However, when she opened the door, he was fast asleep, and rather than disturb him, Lindsay walked out again. Despite his protestations that he was fully recovered, she knew that he was still far from well. It would do him good to sleep. She had had to ring his secretary after lunch to ask her to send some more papers over, and they had had a long chat.

It was her opinion that Lucas was overworking. That she thought very highly of him had been obvious to Lindsay. She had been full of praise for the innovations and improvements he had instituted, and she had also told Lindsay how hard Lucas had worked building up new contacts, and getting new business for the company.

'A lot of our old customers have suffered during the recession,' she had explained, 'and so, of course, we've lost a lot of business which we had during your father's time, but Lucas has worked miracles.'

It was just gone five o'clock when Don reappeared. He and Lindsay had tea together in the sitting room which had always been Sheila's and when he praised the scones with lavish enthusiasm she found it even harder to imagine him as the shrewd hard-headed businessman Lucas had assured her that he was.

At six o'clock she excused herself, explaining that Mrs James was away, and that she was responsible for preparing dinner.

'If it's as good as your scones, I know it's going to be something to look forward to,' he flattered her, adding, 'if you don't mind then I think I'll take a walk down to the village and back.'

At seven o'clock having assured herself that everything was under control in the kitchen Lindsay went upstairs to get changed. Outside Lucas' room she hesitated, colouring up and hating herself for doing so when the door opened inwards unexpectedly and Lucas came out.

'You shouldn't be out of bed,' she told him, trying to recover her equilibrium.

'So how do you intend to keep me there—by joining me?'

Lindsay looked away, her heart jumping up in her throat like a spawning salmon trying to get upriver.

'Dinner will be ready at eight,' she told him stiffly. 'I'm just going to get changed.'

'Lindsay . . .'

She paused and turned to look at him. Just for a moment his expression seemed to soften, and she saw the tiredness at the back of his eyes. Her body ached with her longing to go up to him and soothe the worried lines off his forehead, and she had to curl her fingers into her palm to stop herself from touching him.

'Thanks very much for what you're doing.'

It was the first time he had spoken to her as though she were a normal human being in as long as she could remember—casual words of thanks no more, but they brought a lump to her throat.

To cover herself she shrugged and said brittly, 'Don't mention it—just enter it on my credit side of the books when you're doing the final budget.'

'In other words change my mind about sanctioning your marriage . . .'

'You *can't* sanction my marriage Lucas,' she gritted back at him. 'You don't have that right.'

'I can't forbid the banns—no,' he agreed, 'but refusing to hand over your inheritance is tantamount to the same thing, isn't it Lindsay? *Isn't* it?' He was grasping her shoulders, shaking her almost, his eyes a dark bitter grey as they held hers.

'Why . . . why are you doing this?' She was close to tears, but she didn't want him to see it.

'Why the hell do you think? You're a big girl now,' he reminded her tiredly, 'work it out for yourself.'

She wasn't entirely sure what he meant only that for some reason he was bitterly opposed to her marrying Jeremy; just as he was curtly cynical about everything she did . . . everything she was . . .

'What would happen if you ever fell in love with a man who didn't match up to your father's requirements Lindsay?'

A week ago she would have stated quite calmly that that was impossible, but now she knew the truth. Impelled by a sudden surge of rebellion she tensed beneath his hands and flung back her head so that she could look directly into his eyes. 'If I loved him and he loved me in the same way, then I'd say to hell with my inheritance,' she told him softly.

'And yet given all the passion you just put into that statement, you aren't in love with Jeremy, are you Lindsay?'

'What gives you the right to say that?' She was angry now, defensively angry in case his question led him to the truth. 'You don't know how I feel about him.'

'Like hell I don't,' he told her acidly. His hand slid from her shoulder, to her chin imprisoning it so that she could not look away. His cool scrutiny almost mesmerised her as she stared into the darkness of his eyes.

'*I* haven't forgotten what happened last night Lindsay, and neither have you, even if you would prefer to pretend that you have.'

It was like a blow above her heart, almost totally destroying her. She could feel the blood draining out of her face taking her strength and self control with it.

'You ... you can remember? You ....'

'Of course I can remember,' he mocked her, 'What red blooded man could forget a response like yours, Lindsay.'

'You thought I was Gwen ...' She was babbling now, desperate to protect herself from him. 'I couldn't move away, you were holding me ...'

'What are you trying to do Lindsay? Convince me that we were both playing a game of make-believe? That you thought I was your precious Jeremy?' He smiled with cruel savagery. 'Don't lie to me Lindsay, you knew exactly who I was, and what I was doing ... and you didn't want me to stop either did you ... Did you?' He released her chin to shake her again. The blood roared back through her veins and for a moment she thought she was going to faint.

'Lucas. ... I've got to leave here.' She was barely aware of saying the words, until his hands moved from her shoulders to her waist.

'Oh no you don't,' he denied harshly, 'You're staying here. You're not going to leave me in the lurch now Lindsay ...'

'You can't make me stay here ...'

'No, but your conscience can,' he retorted softly. 'If I don't get this contract, I'll have to put a third of the factory on short time. Is that what you want Lindsay. To be solely responsible for cutting the wages of three hundred men? Not that money, or rather the lack of it ever bothered you. You've got your London apartment and your allowance ... all the lovers and attention you need. Is that what's bugging you now. Physical frustration?'

'No!' She tore herself from his grasp and fled down the landing to her own room. There was no lock on the door, but she knew instinctively that he wouldn't follow her. It seemed an aeon before her pulses had stopped jangling, soothed by the cold water she was running over her wrists. Her face felt hot and flushed, her body prickling with embarrassment and anger.

All day while she had been thinking last night over and forgotten he had known ... He must have been waiting for an opportunity to throw it at her ... and yet somehow he had missed seeing the truth. That puzzled her, and she frowned a little over it. Of course he had the excuse of believing her to be Gwen initially at least; but she had no such excuse. He had accused her of suffering from sexual frustration. Lindsay shrugged, it was stupid to feel so hurt and bitter because he thought she was an experienced woman who had had several lovers. Far better that he thought that than guessed the truth. She couldn't stay here now. But she couldn't leave either, could she? She didn't doubt that he had spoken the truth about the American contract, and if she walked

out now he would have to make explanations to
Don Carter. He would have to book him into an
hotel ... alter all his arrangements. Lindsay
sighed. Lucas was quite blatently using emotional
blackmail to get his own way, but she couldn't call
his bluff ... not if it meant risking the livelihood
of other people.

Somehow or other she managed to get through
serving dinner. There was one moment of
embarrassment during the main course when Don
turned to Lucas and praised her lavishly, adding,
'You're a very lucky man to have such a lovely
wife, Lucas. Mind you take good care of her.
Wives like yours are pretty hard to come by.'

She had forgotten to mention to Lucas that Sam
had mistaken her for Gwen, and now it would be
more awkward than ever to put the other man
right.

She was in the kitchen making the coffee when
Lucas came in. 'What was all that about you being
my wife,' he stressed, coming over to where she
was standing.

'I think he misunderstood when I introduced
myself to him. After all it's a natural enough
mistake. No doubt he was expecting to meet Gwen.
I didn't want to embarrass him by correcting him
in front of the taxi driver, it would have meant
explaining about your divorce and who I am. I
was going to mention it to you earlier and ask you
to put him straight but ...'

'But you didn't,' Lucas supplied sardonically for
her, 'and telling him now is potentially even more
embarrassing. He's going to wonder what the devil
is going on, and why I didn't say something.' He
frowned. 'We'd better just leave it for now. He's

only staying a couple more days,' he was standing only feet away from her and when he moved quickly towards her grasping her shoulders and pulling her back against the lean solidity of his body, Lindsay went rigid with shock. The warm brush of his mouth against the curve of her throat stunned her into silence, despair and pleasure flooding through her in equal measure. She closed her eyes instinctively and only then became aware of footsteps outside the kitchen door. It opened and Don walked in, grinning when he saw them.

'I've just realised I need to make a call to the States. Would it be all right for me to use your 'phone?'

When Lucas assented and released Lindsay to accompany him, he waved him back with a genial smile. 'No, you folks stay right where you are. It's good to see married folks who are still in love enough to want to snatch kisses in the kitchen.'

Lindsay waited until he had gone to round on Lucas, but he wouldn't let her speak, getting in before her, 'I heard him coming,' he told her grimly, 'and since by your folly you've committed us both to this farce that we're married, we might as well give the fiction some substance.'

'There was still no need to ... to touch me,' Lindsay told him stubbornly.

'No need,' Lucas mocked drawling out the words, and lifting his eyebrows in exaggerated disbelief. 'My dear Lindsay, on the contrary, I'd say, if I had to give a name to it, that what you exhibited in my arms last night was a very great need indeed.'

He was going before she could react or respond in any way, leaving her shaking with a mixture of anguish and self-contempt. He had trapped her very neatly, she thought bitterly. He had known that she would never stay within ten miles of him after what had happened last night, so he had deliberately let her believe he didn't remember it—at least until it was too late for her to get away.

But from now on he was going to enjoy taunting her with it ... reminding her of what had happened, and Lindsay didn't know how she was going to endure it.

By the time she went into the drawing room with the coffee Don had finished his 'phone call and was sitting chatting with Lucas.

'I'll leave you two together if you're discussing business,' she said with a smile, glad of the excuse to leave, but as she made to walk past Lucas, his fingers curled round her wrist and he tugged her down beside him on the settee, forcing her to sit so close to him that she could feel the hard muscles of his thigh.

At half-past ten, Don exclaimed that jet lag was getting the better of him and excused himself. Once he had gone Lindsay pulled away from Lucas and went to gather up the coffee cups.

'Out with it,' he commanded, carrying his own over to the tray. 'You're practically bursting with rage. You always did have a ferocious temper.'

'Did I? No wonder with someone like you to contend with,' Lindsay blazed. 'I don't know what you think you're doing, Lucas.'

'Don't you?' He smiled at her with lazy eyes. 'Perhaps, like you, I'm suffering from an acute sense of physical frustration.'

She had not thought of that of course. She knew that he was missing Gwen, but it had never

occurred to her that he might . . . that he . . . She
swallowed hard and stared at him. 'I don't know
what you're suggesting,' she began unevenly . . .
only to be interrupted by his cool, 'Oh come on
Lindsay, stop play-acting, you know exactly what
I'm suggesting,' he told her. The mask of good-
humour suddenly dropped from his face as he
towered over her, all the bones beneath his skin
suddenly compacting making him look exactly
what he was, a ruthlessly angry man. 'Did you
honestly think you could come into my bed, use
me as a substitute for your latest lover, and then
calmly push me on one side? Did you Lindsay?'

He seemed to have some sort of obsession about
her supposed lovers, Lindsay thought hazily. She
had never seen him looking so angry. His grey eyes
burned almost black, hot and dangerous. She
wanted to protest that *he* had been the one to start
it all, but she lacked the courage.

'It wasn't like that.' Her throat had gone dry,
and she licked her lips nervously, quailing under
the sudden bitter, twisting of his mouth as he
watched the betraying gesture. 'For God's sake
don't *do* that.'

In another man his tone might almost have been
described as tortured. This wasn't the Lucas she
knew, Lindsay thought shakily. She had never seen
him so out of control; so much in the grip of his
emotions.

'I won't be used as a substitute for Gwen,
Lucas,' she heard herself saying in a high
unfamiliar voice.

To her astonishment he laughed, the sound
bouncing back off the walls. 'Oh my God,' he said
savagely, 'That's incredible. If only you knew . . .

Don't worry, that's the last thing you're ever likely to be,' he told her cruelly.

The anger suddenly seemed to drain out of him, as he slumped back down into a chair, his face so pale that Lindsay forgot her anger in a surge of protective love. He didn't look well. He *wasn't* well, she reminded herself, leaving the tray to go over to him and touch him tentatively on his arm. 'Lucas . . .'

'Don't do that, damn you,' he swore at her, lurching to his feet. 'I'm going to bed, and if you've any sense at all, you won't try joining me tonight Lindsay.' He saw the look of fear cross her face and laughed cynically. 'Oh come on, don't look at me like that. You're no innocent, and I'm sure at least one of your lovers must have taught you that passion can be at it's best when it's laced very lightly with anger.'

Her body tingled betrayingly as she forced away an immediate image of Lucas kissing her angrily, anger giving way to fierce need . . . to love. To compensate for her moment of weakness, Lindsay turned on him and said coldly, 'I'm afraid we obviously don't share the same tastes, Lucas.'

CHAPTER SEVEN

LINDSAY glanced up from her weeding to look at the study window. Lucas and Don Carter had been in there nearly all morning. Soon it would be time for lunch, but she wasn't sure whether she should disturb them or leave them alone. As she pondered on what to do, the matter was settled for her when Lucas and the American came walking towards her.

She got up smiling easily, and somehow managing to avoid looking directly at Lucas. Why oh why did her heart have to start thumping so painfully and so betrayingly, just because he was within touching distance?

'I was just wondering what to do about lunch,' she told them both. 'Are you ready to eat now, or . . .'

'We're ready.'

Lucas sounded so terse that Lindsay wondered if his talks with Don had perhaps not gone very well, but this fear was banished when Don added warmly, 'but tonight you must both let me take you out for dinner. No I insist,' he continued firmly when Lucas would have interrupted. 'It can be a "thank-you" as well as a celebration.' He turned to beam at Lindsay. 'Your husband and I have just come to some mutually beneficial business agreements, and if you could suggest somewhere reasonably local where I could take you both out to dinner this evening . . .'

'No, please ... you really ...' Lindsay began hesitantly, sensing that Lucas did not want the American to take them out. Probably because he didn't want to be seen with her, she thought bitterly, but all her hesitancy was in vain. Don Carter insisted that he intended to take them out and in the end, it was Lucas, who suggested, in a curt voice that a little known, but very good hotel some fifty miles away might be a suitable venue.

It was after lunch before Lindsay saw Lucas alone. He came into the kitchen while she was loading the dishwasher, frowning angrily.

For some reason his presence in the kitchen disturbed her. For *some* reason? She mocked her own feeble attempt to deceive herself. She knew exactly why she found him so disturbing, and painful though it was, sooner or later she was going to have to come to terms with the fact that she loved him—come to terms with it and overcome it. She shivered slightly hating herself for her weakness and, in some strange way, angry with Lucas because he was the root cause of it. Her anger manifested itself in a distinct tartness in her voice as she claimed, 'Anyone would think from looking at you that your business negotiations had failed—not succeeded.' Inwardly she was taut with pain; with the knowledge that no matter how successful he might be professionally the fact that he had lost Gwen outweighed any pleasure he might gain from his business successes. How could she bear knowing how much he loved the other woman and how little he loved her? She would bear it because she *must*, she told herself drably. There was no other way. After all she was scarcely the first woman in the world to suffer from unrequited love, and doubtless she was a long way from being the last.

She came out of her sombre thoughts to find Lucas glowering at her. 'In case it's escaped your attention we could have a potentially embarrassing situation on our hands this evening.'

Lindsay stared at him, not really understanding what he meant.

'This meal Don is insistent on us having,' he told her with curt impatience. 'Why do you think I suggested so far away, or have you forgotten already, that Don still believes you're my wife?'

The harsh bitterness in Lucas voice, jolted her into reality. Of course she had forgotten. No wonder Lucas had been so reluctant to let Sam take them out for a meal. If they went anywhere local they'd be bound to be recognised. She bit her lip, cursing her own lack of foresight.

'Why the hell didn't you try harder to put him off?' Lucas demanded.

'I . . .' For some stupid reason tears pricked the back of her eyes. She turned away hoping that Lucas had not seen them. What was the matter with her?

'Oh what the hell,' Lucas muttered tiredly, 'We'll just have to hope that we don't bump into anyone we know, or that if we do, it doesn't come out that Sam believes we're married.'

'It's a natural enough mistake to make,' Lindsay protested, 'and after all we are brother and sister . . .'

'Like hell we are.' The savagery in his voice made her shrink back from him, freezing motionless, as he strode out of the kitchen, slamming the door behind him.

She had never seen Lucas like this before. When she had been a teenager he had been so patient with her. At least until Gwen's arrival into his life, and even then he had treated her with cool indifference, never this hot, almost uncontrollable anger that seemed to have its roots in some inner agony she could only guess at.

The altercation with Lucas left her feeling weak and tensely overwrought. He and Don were still engaged in business discussions and on impulse Lindsay decided she might as well drive into their small local market town. She could have her hair done and browse in the local shops, it might take her mind off all her emotional problems.

She was just about to get into the car when Lucas and Don walked out of the front door.

'We're just going out to the factory for an hour,' Lucas told her, frowning as he realised she too was going out.

'Where are you going?' The question was brusque enough to make Don look rather curiously at him.

'Just into Malden,' Lindsay told him quickly, 'I . . . I've got some shopping to do, and I wanted to call in and see Tom. Tom Henry was her father's solicitor and along with Lucas, her other trustee. She had invented the excuse of going to see him on impulse, not wanting Lucas to read anything into the fact that she was planning to have her hair done. She felt so self conscious about her feelings for him that she was petrified she might somehow betray them, and yet as the dark look crossed his face she knew that she had said the wrong thing. There wasn't time to retract her statement though,

as Lucas was already heading in the direction of
his own car.

Why should the fact that she was going to call in
and see Tom make him look so angry? she
wondered wryly as she started her car. Tom was
more of an honorary uncle to her than a mere
solicitor, and she always tried to call and see him
when she was home.

Half an hour later she was parking her car in the
small town square. She had always loved Malden
with its old stone buildings; many dating back to
medieval times. In the days when this part of the
world had been famous for its wool, Malden had
been a bustling wealthy little town, and these days
its inhabitants took great pride in its history. Here
and there a Georgian façade mingled with the
older Tudor buildings, and it was in one of these
tall Georgian fronted buildings that Tom's offices
were.

She went to see him first, and was welcomed
warmly by his secretary, whom she had known
since schooldays.

'Lindsay, my dear, come in and sit down,' Tom
Henry smiled affectionately at her. He was
genuinely fond of his late client's daughter. He
knew of her father's hopes and plans for her, and
while he had wisely never interfered, it was his
private feeling that he had been wrong to bring
Lindsay up in the belief that she owed it to him to
marry as he wished. On one or two occasions he
had attempted very gently to point this out to his
client but the other man had been so stubbornly
insistent that he knew what was best for his
daughter that Tom had backed down. And yet
despite all his stubbornness, Tom knew that

ultimately her father would have wanted whatever gave Lindsay the greatest happiness. It was just unfortunate that his own experience had left him with such an intense need to show the class he thought had rejected him that he was every bit as good as they were. Which of course he had been.

'Tea?' Tom offered his guest, as she sat down. Now that he could see her properly he was worried by the dark shadows haunting her eyes, and the extreme slenderness of her body.

Lindsay accepted his offer, and sat silently while he rang through to ask Mary to bring them some tea.

'Is it business or pleasure that brings you to see me?' he asked at last, when Mary had poured their tea and left them.

'A little of both,' Lindsay admitted, remembering how often as a teenager she had come to Tom with her problems. He had been a good friend to her then, a wise, avuncular figure whom she had sometimes found more approachable than her own father.

'You're too thin,' Tom told her, urging her to take a piece of shortbread, 'and you look tired.'

Lindsay smiled, shrugging aside his concern. 'You know how it is, the pace of life is so hectic these days.'

'Only if you allow it to be,' Tom told her drily, 'You have no need to live and work in London, Lindsay. Your father's will stipulates that you receive a generous income from his estate . . .'

'You mean I could have stayed at home and lived a life of leisure.' She shook her head grimacing faintly. 'Lucas wouldn't have wanted that . . . especially not after he and Gwen married.'

She looked up just in time to catch a rather strange expression crossing Tom's face, and frowned quickly, asking, 'Tom what is it?'

'Nothing . . . nothing at all my dear.' He seemed to be examining his nails rather thoroughly and Lindsay had the feeling that there was something he was not telling her.

'I know that Lucas and Gwen are divorced,' she said hesitantly at last. 'It came as rather a shock, especially as Lucas hadn't let me know . . . In fact I had no idea until I came down here that their marriage was over.'

The pain inside her flooded out into her voice, and Tom frowned. 'No doubt Lucas had his reasons.'

'I couldn't believe it when he said Gwen had been the one to . . . to be unfaithful to him. She . . . she wanted him so badly I . . . Lucas is missing her dreadfully.'

Again she was surprised by the look that crossed the solicitor's face. 'I suppose you handled the divorce for Lucas,' she added, without knowing quite what had made her ask.

'Not personally,' Tom told her. 'We're an old fashioned firm, Lindsay, and we don't handle divorce work, but I was able to recommend to Lucas an old friend of mine in London who specialises in marital law . . . But let's talk about pleasanter things,' he suggested. 'What are your plans for the future.'

Here was her chance to talk to him about her marriage to Jeremy, to tell him how difficult and contrary Lucas was being, and yet as she sat there, watching motes of dust dance in the sunlight that shafted through the square paned windows, she now knew that no matter what the future held she could not marry Jeremy. Admitting as much to herself lifted a great weight of guilt and uncertainty from her heart. No matter how suitable Jeremy might have been from her father's point of view, Lindsay knew that she could not marry him, or anyone like him. If she couldn't have Lucas, then she didn't want anyone. Half of her mocked her for her feelings and yet the other half applauded her. Better to settle for nothing than to marry a man whom in her heart of hearts she knew she did not love. Sooner or later she would begin to resent Jeremy because he was not Lucas ... and he would sense it and resent her. For years she had told herself that she owed it to her father to try and please him and yet suddenly she knew that for all that time she had been trying to mould herself into a pattern that wasn't her. Jeremy was nice enough ... she enjoyed his company ... but she didn't like his parents, and she didn't care either for their values—values which she would be expected to pass on to her own children. All her life she had tried to be what her father wanted, and now suddenly she knew that she had been wrong. She should have had the courage to stand up to him during his lifetime—to tell him that she could not live out his dreams for him.

Watching the expressions chase one another across her face, Tom sighed inwardly. One could not practise his profession and not become something of a student of human nature. He loved Lindsay almost as though she were his own child, and on many occasions he had had to bite on his tongue to stop himself from criticising what her father had done to her, albeit with the best motives in the world. He had truly sympathised with his old friend, sharing his grief at the loss of his young wife; resenting on his behalf the family which had cut themselves off from their only child when she chose to marry outside their social circle. But times changed, and it had been wrong of Charles to want to use Lindsay as he had.

'No plans,' Lindsay said at last, answering his question. 'I have a good job which I enjoy and that's enough for me at the moment.' She bit her lip and stared out of the window before saying softly. 'Tom ... would you think me very disloyal if I said that I'm not going to be able to do what daddy wanted me to?'

'You mean you're not going to be able to marry a man your father would have approved of?'

'Something like that,' Lindsay admitted wryly. 'Oh, I did think I could. In fact I was all set to announce my engagement, but ...'

'But you discovered you loved Lucas instead,' Tom supplied mildly for her.

Lindsay went white and then red, staring at him without being able to formulate a single word, until she managed to stammer. 'How ... how did you know?'

'You forget how long I've known you Lindsay,' Tom told her gently. 'I guessed a long time ago how you felt about Lucas, but I think I'm right in saying you've only just discovered yourself how you feel?'

'This weekend,' Lindsay admitted. 'I came down to tell him I was planning to get engaged. We had the most awful row about it, and then Lucas became ill ...'

'And you realised how you really feel about him?' Tom supplemented quietly. 'My dear girl what can I say? I've always thought your father was wrong to bring you up as he did—that's not to say I didn't sympathise with him. He adored your mother you know, and it angered and hurt him that she should die just when he was in a position to give her all the things she'd given up for him.'

'But Mummy didn't care about that. She loved him for what he was.'

'I know that my dear, but grief does weird things to people. It made your father yearn to be revenged on those who, in his eyes, had helped to cause your mother's death by rejecting her. And I'm afraid he used you as an instrument of that revenge.'

'Partially my own fault. I wanted to please him so much . . . I should have stood up to him more, told him. . . . Lucas was the only person he would ever really listen to. In fact I used to think that Lucas was on my side, but after Daddy died. . . .'

'He was in a very difficult position my dear. Try to remember that at the time he was struggling to keep your father's business empire going. When your father died the city panicked a little . . . there was talk of the company folding without your father there to run it. Of course Lucas has proved since then how admirably he was able to step into your father's shoes. Your father himself knew that. He had the highest regard for Lucas you know.

'Yes I do,' Lindsay acknowledged. 'In fact there were times in my early teens when I was almost jealous of Lucas. He seemed to get on so well with Daddy . . . to share things with him that I couldn't. I often used to think that Daddy wished Lucas had been his son and not just his stepson.'

'Yes, I think possibly you're right, although that doesn't detract from the love your father had for you. You were always very special to him Lindsay, and he loved you very much.

'I think in Lucas he saw himself as a young man, but with the rough corners smoothed off. And Lucas cared very deeply for your father too . . . as he does for you.'

'No.' Lindsay shook her head firmly. 'No . . . you're wrong there . . . Why he couldn't wait to try and marry me off once Daddy had died and then when he married Gwen . . . Well let's just say neither of them went out of their way to make me feel exactly welcome.'

Tom sighed a little at the bitterness in her voice. 'My dear, try to understand,' he appealed to her. 'Try to see it as an outsider might. You and Lucas were virtually living alone together. . . Oh I know you're going to tell me that he is your stepbrother . . . but there was no blood tie . . . no real relationship that Lucas could hold up to the world to stop it from gossiping, and people did gossip. There were plenty of people locally who were ready to suspect the worst of Lucas. After all, in their eyes at least, there was nothing to stop him from marrying you himself and thus safeguarding your father's wealth for his own use.'

'But I was barely seventeen . . . I . . .'

'And Lucas was a good deal older. Looking back it's difficult to know what alternative he had other than to marry and provide you with a chaperon, so to speak.'

'Gwen couldn't wait to get me out of the house,'

Lindsay laughed bitterly, 'she even accused me of wanting Lucas for myself.' A shadow crossed her face. 'I used to think that she was wrong, but now . . . One thing I do know now is that if I do ever marry it will be because I'm so much in love that I can't bear not to—not for any other reason.'

'Good, I'm very glad to hear of it. Don't ever think that you mustn't marry because your choice of husband might not have been your father's approval. People change and adapt. Who's to say that your father's views would not have mellowed in time? I'm sure that at heart he would have wanted your happiness more than he wanted his own revenge. He would never really have wanted you to marry simply to please him, not after the happiness he had shared with your mother, and you must always remember that.'

'I will.' Lindsay stood up and kissed his cheek. 'Thanks for listening to me . . . but somehow I don't think I shall be marrying now.' She frowned a little. 'At least Lucas will be pleased to hear my engagement's off . . . He wasn't at all keen on the idea. I don't know why. Time was when he couldn't wait to marry me off.'

'Perhaps you should try asking him,' Tom suggested mildly. 'People who ask questions have been known occasionally to get answers.'

Lindsay grimaced. 'Not this time. In fact the mood Lucas has been in with me these last few days, I should think he'd take great pleasure in not answering me. I can't understand why I should feel about him the way I do. It's not as if my love is ever likely to be returned. I never realised how much he cared for Gwen . . . I can't understand why she left him either . . .'

'Try not to worry so much,' Tom advised her. 'Things have a way of working out if you just let them.'

'The mills of God?' Lindsay murmured wryly. 'Perhaps you're right. After all I haven't exactly had a roaring success doing things my way.'

After she had left the solicitor's office Lindsay went into the hairdressers she used to patronise when she lived at home. The girl who owned the salon remembered her, and assured her that they were able to fit her in.

'I've always envied you being a natural blonde,' she confided to Lindsay when she had been shampooed and was seated in front of a mirror. 'Is it for a special occasion or just a pick-me-up?'

'I'm going out to dinner tonight,' Lindsay told her, 'Nothing too fancy though.'

'Umm, very nice. Where are you going? Anywhere local?'

They chatted easily while she worked on Lindsay's hair, and sitting in the familiar surroundings Lindsay succumbed to a wave of nostalgia. How she had hated London when she first moved there. She had ached to run back home, but her pride would not let her. Even then she must have known she loved Lucas, but she had hidden the truth from herself, too proud and frightened to admit it. Jeremy wasn't going to be pleased when she gave him the news that their engagement was off. She sighed faintly. What was wrong with her. Why couldn't she be like countless hundreds of other women and settle quite happily for second best? She didn't know the answer to her own question, only that she was sure that for her it would not work out. Her body and her heart would always ache for Lucas, and she would never be able to make anyone else an even halfway satisfactory wife while that was the case.

She got back to the house ten minutes or so before Lucas and Don returned. She witnessed their arrival from her bedroom window, for some reason stepping back automatically as Lucas chanced to glance upwards. He couldn't have been looking for her and therefore it was ridiculous to feel her heart pounding in this quite adolescent way. He still looked grimly angry and she thought wryly that the evening ahead did not promise to be a particularly pleasant one.

She went downstairs to join the two men, producing tea and scones for Don who told her that he was thinking of importing the tradition of English four o'clock tea into his own life-style.

'In fact, if she wasn't already your wife, I'd be trying to persuade this lovely lady to come back with me,' he told Lucas. 'She is very definitely one of a kind.'

'That she is,' Lindsay heard Lucas mutter, and she had to stop herself from crying out in pain at the bitterness in his voice. If he couldn't love her, surely he could like her instead of treating her with this bitter hostility. What had she ever done to make him react to her like this unless it was simply that she wasn't Gwen?

At six o'clock she excused herself to go upstairs and get changed. She had already decided what to wear; a simple black sheath of a dress in matt jersey, which she knew suited her. It was very plain with a round neck and long sleeves, but the fluid jersey clung to her body, embracing every curve; it was a dress that was sensual without being showily sexy, and knowing that she looked good in it, lent her the confidence she so desperately needed.

She arrived downstairs on the dot of seven to find Lucas already in the drawing room, nursing a tumbler of amber liquid.

'Oh it's all right,' he told her with the savagery she was now coming to recognise. 'I don't intend to get drunk. I'll be driving for one thing.'

'And for another?' Lindsay prompted, aware of his hostility and determined not to be unnerved by it.

'Well let's just say a masochistic streak in me urges me to deny myself its anaesthetic properties in favour of suffering pain in the hope that the exercise might prove ultimately beneficial.'

Lindsay wasn't quite sure what he meant. Was it the pain of losing Gwen that he wanted to anaesthetise himself against? If so what good could forcing himself to endure it do?

She was saved from having to reply by Don's entrance. 'Say that's a real attractive gown you're wearing,' he complimented Lindsay sincerely, 'but not as attractive as the lady inside it. Your wife sure has good taste,' he told Lucas admiringly.

'She certainly does.'

She was so surprised by the warmth in Lucas' voice that she turned to stare at him. 'After all she chose to marry me,' Lucas added with a brief smile. 'Proof positive that you're right.'

Both men laughed and Lindsay forced herself to join in. She was dreading the evening ahead, and already had the beginnings of a headache. Coward, she condemned herself, grimly following the men out to the car.

The hotel Lucas had recommended to Don was

one Lindsay was not particularly familiar with. Her father had always preferred to eat at home, and on the rare occasions when dates had taken her out it had always been to more local and less exclusive places. She had dined in expensive restaurants in London of course—Jeremy liked to be seen in the right places. Jeremy! Guilt stabbed her. How furious he would be when she told him her decision, and who could blame him. After all he had not rushed her, she had known when she agreed to marry him that she did not love him. But she had not known that she *did* love Lucas. And that was something she could never tell Jeremy.

The small, elegant dining room was half full when they were shown in. They had been given a table by the window, overlooking the gardens which were illuminated with Japanese flares.

'Very nice,' Don approved, as they sat down. 'I suppose this place was once a private house.'

While the two men were talking Lindsay looked round, tensing suddenly as she recognised the foursome sitting at a nearby table.

'Something wrong?'

She was surprised that Lucas had noticed her tension. She had thought she had herself well under control.

'No ... no, everything's fine,' but even as she spoke her eyes were drawn once more to the quartet seated nearby. She had recognised them instantly. The older pair were neighbours of Jeremy's parents; the young man she didn't recognise, but the girl was their daughter, and Jeremy's mother had made little secret of the fact that Amelia Rhodes was everything she had always hoped for in a daughter-in-law. Amelia saw her and gave her a distant little smile. Lindsay's heart sank. She and Amelia had never managed to get on. Lindsay was all too conscious of the fact that until she came along Amelia had considered Jeremy her property. A year or two younger than Lindsay, she tended to react like a spoilt little girl whenever she couldn't get her own way. Her parents were wealthy and part of the set in which Jeremy's parents moved. All in all marriage to Amelia was exactly what they had planned for their son. Until she came along ... Whoever the young man with them was, it was obvious to Lindsay that Amelia wasn't paying him too much attention. After looking at and then dismissing Lindsay her eyes had remained fixed on Lucas' tall, broad shouldered frame, with a look in them that Lindsay had instantly recognised. She felt acutely sick with jealousy and nerves. How dare Amelia look at Lucas like that her emotions raged, even while she knew she was being ridiculous. What right did she have to feel jealous? None! None at all.

She gave her order to the waiter mechanically, trying to force some enthusiastic response to Don's conversation, but all the time her attention was really focused on Amelia Rhodes.

'You're looking like someone who's just discovered they've lost a fortune on the stock exchange,' Lucas told her tersely between courses while Don was chatting earnestly to their waiter. 'What the hell's the matter.'

'Nothing. . . .'

The word had barely left her lips when she saw Amelia swaying towards them on heels that were too high, and which were teamed with a dress that was far too tight for her plumpish five-foot-nothing frame, Lindsay thought waspishly.

As she had known she would the other girl stopped by their table, avid blue eyes darting from Lindsay's pale face to Lucas' remote one.

'Lindsay darling, what a surprise,' she exclaimed with false sweetness, 'Aren't you going to introduce me?'

Stifling the cold feeling of doom spreading through her stomach Lindsay performed the introductions, trying to stem the wild tide of jealousy searing her as Lucas openly assessed Amelia's feminine curves. He was a free man and could do whatever he chose, she reminded herself but it didn't make the pain abate one little bit.

'Are you enjoying your stay here in our country Mr Carter,' Amelia cooed at Don. The girl was impossible Lindsay thought angrily. She couldn't resist flirting with any male.

'I sure am,' responded Don genially. 'Lucas here and his pretty wife have made me more than welcome.'

'His wife?' Pencilled eyebrows shot upwards as Amelia stared at Lindsay. 'My dear, I had no idea, Poor Jeremy . . . When . . .'

'Amelia, your dinner is going cold.'

Mrs Rhodes' frosty inclination of her head in Lindsay's direction recalled Amelia's attention to her waiting parents and boyfriend. With another openly inviting look at Lucas, she drifted back to her own table.

Even though she had gone, Lindsay couldn't recover her equilibrium. Her hands shook when she picked up her knife and fork and she laid them back down again, her appetite completely gone.

Dear God, why on earth did the Rhodes' have to be dining here of all places, and tonight?

Amelia would lose no time in telling her mother of her supposed marriage to Lucas, and Mrs Rhodes was bound to mention it to Jeremy's mother. Her body went cold as she thought through the complications that would then ensue. Tomorrow morning she would have to return to London and speak to Jeremy. Telling him that their engagement was off was not something she could do over the telephone.

'Lindsay?'

The sharply compelling tone of Lucas' voice brought her back to the present.

'I'm sorry. I'm just a little bit tired,' she apologised, aware of Lucas' sharply angry, and Don's concerned glances on her. 'I had a headache when we came out and it seems to be getting worse.'

'My dear you should have said.' Don was instantly sympathetic. 'We'll leave right away ... I ...'

'No ... no, please ...' Lindsay was anxious to make as little fuss as possible. 'It isn't that bad.'

She wasn't entirely surprised when the Rhodes' family stopped by their table on their way out of the restaurant.

'Lindsay ...' Mrs Rhodes' manner was aloofly distant, and no attempt was made to introduce her to Amelia's male companion, but Lindsay was left in no doubt that Mrs Rhodes had taken in every detail of her appearance, and that of Lucas, and she suspected that they would be faithfully reported to Jeremy's mother at the first opportunity.

She waited until they were back home to tell Lucas that she intended to go to London the next day. He had followed her into the kitchen when she had offered to make them all a nightcap, and Lindsay could tell from one look at his set expression that he was not pleased.

'Why? Frightened that the boyfriend might run off with someone else?'

What would he say if she told him that she couldn't care less what Jeremy did? Just for a moment Lindsay allowed her imagination full rein, swiftly quelling the impulse to tell him and to tell him exactly why she could no longer marry anyone else. Don't be a fool, she warned herself angrily. What does he care what you feel about him. He still loves Gwen.

'Come back Lindsay.' The soft violence in his voice brought her out of her thoughts, her breath catching in her throat as she looked up into his dark face. 'Why did you go to see Tom this afternoon?' he demanded. 'Why, Lindsay? Was it to ask him to break my trusteeship?'

Dimly Lindsay remembered threatening to do just that, but surely Lucas didn't really think? Astonishment suspended her ability to speak. She could only stare up at him, until some small spark of self-preservation made her say huskily, 'And what if I did? You have no right to try to stop me from marrying Jeremy, Lucas.'

'No right, but every reason,' she thought she heard him mutter as he turned and swung out of the kitchen, but she couldn't be sure she had heard him accurately, and it was impossible to understand exactly what he meant without questioning him. Despite Tom's advice she was still a long,

long way from demanding Lucas' answers to any of her questions. Because she feared them? Very probably she thought tiredly, trying to stroke the tension away from her temples and concentrate instead on what she was doing.

CHAPTER EIGHT

SHE woke up with the awareness of something unpleasant hanging over her, although it took two or three seconds for her tired brain to relay to her exactly what it was. She had to go up to London and see Jeremy.

Her headache had increased rather than abated, and she hadn't slept well. Stop trying to avoid the issue, she warned herself as she showered and dressed. There was no longer even any excuse for her to remain. Don was flying back to New York that afternoon, and Lucas was now well over his bout of fever. She would have *had* to return to London anyway.

Breakfast was a sombre meal with Don saying openly that he would miss them both when he returned home. For all his business success, Lindsay got the feeling that he was essentially a lonely man; much as she would be a lonely woman from now on. Would Caroline still want to share a flat with her once she had finished with Jeremy, or would loyalty to her cousin necessitate her moving out? One thing at a time Lindsay warned herself. One thing at a time.

After breakfast Don went upstairs to pack. He had arranged for a taxi to pick him up he told Lucas when the latter offered to drive him to Heathrow. Lindsay too had packing to do, and when she had cleared away the breakfast things she went upstairs to make a start on it. She had

decided that she would leave after lunch which
would give her plenty of time to get to London
before the evening rush hour.

Don left at eleven o'clock. 'You must both come
to the States and stay with me,' he insisted, and
Lindsay felt terrible agreeing. If only she had
corrected his mistake on that first morning. But
she had not done so, and what had happened since
was entirely her own fault.

When his taxi had disappeared she went inside
to ring the flat to warn Caroline to expect her, but
the other girl must have been out because there
was no reply.

Having finished her packing Lindsay decided to
have a shower and change before leaving. She had
just stepped out of the shower when she heard a
car outside. Grabbing a towel and wrapping it
round her still damp body she hurried to the
window, horrified to see Jeremy, walking purpose-
fully towards the house. One look at his face
warned her that Amelia had not been slow to pass
on her news, and Lindsay almost ran across her
room and downstairs in her haste to intercept
Jeremy before Lucas saw him.

As she hurried downstairs she slipped and fell,
bumping into a small table and knocking it over.
The noise was worse than her injuries, and it
brought Lucas out of the study, his forehead
creased in a frown that deepened when he saw her
sprawled on the stairs.

'What the devil . . .'

'I fell,' Lindsay interrupted weakly at the same
moment as the doorbell pealed, wishing that Lucas
would not stand quite so close to her. His fingers
closed round her arm, and he half pulled her to her

feet. She winced as her ankle refused to support her weight properly and the doorbell pealed again.

'It's Jeremy,' Lindsay told him huskily, 'He must have heard about last night. Amelia's parents are very friendly with his,' she explained tiredly, 'In fact I suspect his mother really wanted him to marry Amelia, and I'm sure her mother will have lost no time in informing her that I'm now "married" to you.'

She saw his mouth compress as he looked from her too pale face to the door, and then abruptly he bent down and picked her up, carrying her back upstairs, pausing only to call over his shoulder, 'The door's open—come in.'

Jeremy must have heard him because he walked in just in time to see Lucas going upstairs with her.

'My God,' he swore hoarsely, the colour flooding from his face as he stared up at them. 'So it's true . . .'

'Jeremy, no . . . We're not married. . . . Lucas, put me down please,' Lindsay pleaded. 'Jeremy, I was coming back today to see you . . .'

'Yes, I'm sure you were,' he was sneering up at her now. 'Such a pity Amelia spotted you last night, otherwise you could have gone on eating your cake and keeping it for ever, couldn't you? How long has it been going on Lindsay?' he demanded bitterly, 'How long have you and Armitage been lovers? Since your father died? No wonder his wife left him. My mother warned me that something was going on, but I wouldn't listen to her. Lindsay isn't like that, I told her . . . And you weren't were you—for me. No wonder you managed to play the little innocent so successfully for me . . . you were getting all the sex you wanted elsewhere weren't you?'

'No ... no ... it wasn't like that. Jeremy, please, you've got to listen.' She was crying now as much with shock as with pain. She had never seen Jeremy like this before; never seen this sarcastic, bitter side of him. 'Lucas, put me down,' she urged. 'Let me speak to Jeremy. . . .'

Instead of releasing her she felt the muscles in his arms tense as he reinforced his hold of her. 'What's the point in that,' he drawled, shocking her into silence. 'I should think it's self evident how we feel about one another.'

How they felt ... Lindsay felt as though all the breath had been knocked out of her body. She turned in his arms and looked straight into his eyes. They looked mockingly back at her, registering every emotion she was suffering. His fingers traced the line of her arm, disturbing the fine hairs and making them stand on end as a frisson of sexual awareness shivered through her. 'There's no point in keeping it secret any more . . .'

'But you don't ... we're not ...'

'I suppose you were going to üse me as a convenient smoke screen to hide your affair behind,' Jeremy continued still watching them. 'Ask yourself why he doesn't make an honest woman out of you Lindsay. After all he's free to now, isn't he? And to think I fell for that sob story about him being ill ... about his wife leaving him. Some fool you took me for. I should have known what was going on. You always were such a cold bitch towards me. I couldn't believe it when Amelia rang me up last night and told me she'd seen you and that you'd been passing yourself off as Mrs Armitage. Quite a cozy arrangement as far as you're concerned,' he sneered at Lucas, adding viciously, 'Well you're . . . Well you're welcome to her. I wouldn't marry her if she had three times her father's fortune coming to her after this.'

'Jeremy please . . . Lucas, tell him it isn't true . . .' her voice was raw and painful, hot tears stinging her eyes as Jeremy turned and walked through the door. As though he sensed her desire to run after him Lucas tightened his hold of her, gripping her almost painfully until the sound of Jeremy's car had died away completely.

'Why?' she asked dispiritedly into the heavy silence that followed. 'Why did you let him think we were lovers?'

'Why not? It seemed to be what he wanted to think. Come on Lindsay,' he said roughly when she didn't speak. 'The man was looking for an escape hatch. Surely even you could see that. He didn't want to marry you,' he told her brutally, 'and he certainly didn't love you.'

'Love? And just what would you know about that?' Lindsay spat back at him, too angry to care how much she was hurting him. Why hadn't he told Jeremy the truth? Why did he hate her so much that he had had to humiliate her like that? She didn't care really what Jeremy thought of her. If he could believe so badly of her so easily then she was well rid of him, but it pained her to know that Lucas would let someone speak to her like that, especially when none of it was true.

'One hell of a lot more than *you* apparently,' Lucas told her. The softly threatening drawl was back in his voice, and Lindsay felt herself tensing. 'Well Lindsay,' he probed relentlessly. 'Was it true?'

'Was what true?' she asked listlessly, wishing he

would put her down and then she could escape to
the privacy of her own room.

'Jeremy implied that you'd never been lovers.
Have you?'

Anger, hot and corrosive welled up inside her.
She wanted to lash out at someone and Lucas was
the only person within reach, but nothing she
could do would hurt him, only herself.

'Well?' he demanded.

What did he want to know for? So that he could
taunt her about that as well?

'No . . . no . . . Jeremy and I have never been
lovers! No one has ever been my lover. There now,
are you satisfied? Any more questions?'

She took advantage of his momentary relaxation
to thrust herself out of his arms. Thankfully now
her ankle supported her, as she hobbled up the
remaining stairs, tugging the towel more securely
around herself.

Safely inside her room she slammed the door
and then leaned against it breathing deeply. That
surely couldn't really have been shock and yes,
despair she had seen in Lucas' eyes when she flung
the truth at him could it? Well if he felt guilty it
served him right. He shouldn't have been so quick
to condemn her; to think the worst of her. What
would it have mattered to him anyway if she had
had lovers, she wondered restlessly. He couldn't
care less what she did with her life, or who she
shared it with. Wrong, an inner voice corrected
her. He had cared enough not to want her to
marry Jeremy. But why? What could he possibly
have against Jeremy?

Her towel felt damp against her chilled skin, and
Lindsay threw it tiredly across the room. She

would put it in the linen basket later. Right now all she wanted to do was to get dressed and leave. She didn't think her nervous system could stand any more scenes like the one she had just endured. She had never dreamed that Amelia would get in touch with Jeremy direct, or that Jeremy would drive down here to confront her. Perhaps it was better to leave things as they stood. Telling Jeremy the truth now would not achieve anything, and would he believe her anyway? The faint click of her bedroom door opening barely registered as Lindsay stood deep in thought.

'Lindsay I . . .'

She moved away from the protective shadow of her bathroom door at the same moment as Lucas stepped into her room, both of them suddenly tense and silent, Lindsay because she was acutely aware of her nudity, and Lucas, apparently because he was transfixed by the sight of her. She wanted to turn and run, but pride would not let her. Unconsciously her chin lifted, and Lindsay met his scrutiny determined not to be embarrassed by it.

'Looking for some physical flaw to justify my virginal state?' she managed to say lightly at last.

'Flaw?' He lifted his gaze from her body, and for the first time since she could remember Lindsay saw that his eyes were not really focusing on hers. He looked dazed almost, his face oddly pale, his body, now that she looked properly at him, tense, braced as though against a blow.

'Flawed? You?' He came towards her, standing so close to her that she could have touched him if she lifted her hand. 'Lindsay, you're the most perfectly feminine human being I've ever seen.'

The reverence in his voice stunned her. She

looked into his eyes expecting to see mockery there, but instead all she could see was a need that made her blink and wonder if she could really believe her own eyes.

'And you of course are an expert.' She forced herself to inject a mocking note into her voice, willing herself not to betray how shaken and disturbed she was. Her robe lay on the bed, and if she moved away from him she could pick it up and put it on. Half of her badly wanted to, and yet the other half ... she shivered violently, suppressing a shocked exclamation in her throat as Lucas reached out and touched her, his hand sliding smoothly over her skin, his fingers exploring the sensitivity of her flesh as he stroked upwards over her hip, following the narrow indentation of her waist, her rib cage and then the outer swell of her breast. Her body shook with reaction, and she had no need to look down to be aware of her body's own open betrayal of her feelings.

'Lindsay!'

It was as though both of them were gripped by the same spell, and unable to break free from it. They were the same two people they had always been and yet they were different. This Lucas who touched her and trembled as he did so was a different Lucas from the one who derided and hurt her with the scathing lash of his tongue, just as this Lindsay who melted and yielded in open supplication of that same touch was a different Lindsay from the one who had so jealously hidden her feelings.

'Lindsay.' Lucas leaned forward, framing her face with his hands, her name a prayer on his lips before he touched them gently to her own. His

mouth explored hers as lightly and delicately as a
butterfly touching the fragile petals of a flower. At
any time she chose Lindsay knew she could draw
back, but that *wasn't* what she wanted. In
wonderment, she let Lucas explore the softness of
her mouth, her senses so acutely attuned to his
that she knew long before the pressure of his kiss
increased what he wanted from her.

Her arms slid round his neck bringing her body
into closer contact with him. The hard wall of his
chest crushed her breasts and yet the sensation
wasn't unpleasant. Her mouth opened beneath the
insistent pressure of his and when his hands
moulded her body against his own and she became
aware of his male arousal she moaned softly in her
throat, pressing herself more closely against him,
abandoning herself to the surging tides of desire
running swiftly through them both.

Time and reason were both suspended, reality
fading away to be replaced by a world where the
senses alone reigned. Later, Lindsay couldn't
remember them moving towards the bed, only the
erotic delicacy of Lucas' lips exploring the long
length of her legs, the vulnerable area behind her
knee where the warmth of his breath made her
body pulse and the blood race through her veins.

'Lucas...' Shivering with pleasure she reached
down to touch him, winding her fingers through
his hair and then gasping his name in hectic
urgency as his body covered hers and his hands
cupped and stroked the aching tenderness of her
breasts.

Unable to bear the sexual tension he was
arousing inside her, her hand slid inside his shirt,
stroking the hard bones of his shoulders. His

tongue stroked her nipples and she arched back,
panting in short breaths of exquisite delight, her
eyes enormous in the pale triangle of her face as
she watched his head descend to the proferred
enticement of her breasts, his tongue teasing her
taut nipples until she cried out his name and
clutched at his hair. The slight grate of his teeth
against the tender aureole of her breast was
shatteringly erotic, stimulating her into arching
wildly beneath him, mutely imploring a deeper
possession than that offered by the delicate
movement of his mouth feathering across her
breasts, and her breath seemed to lodge in a
painful lump in her throat when Lucas responded
to the physical enticement she was helpless to stop,
by cupping her breast and drawing her nipple
deeply into his mouth sucking rhythmically on her
tender flesh until she could feel the fierce thud of
his heart as it beat into her skin, and her own teeth
were nipping wantonly at the corded strength of
his neck, as she sought relief from the desperate
need he was arousing inside her.

'Lindsay . . .' When he finally released her, his
skin was as flushed as it had been when he had
been in the grip of his fever, his eyes almost black
as they scrutinised, possessively, the havoc he had
wrought on her body.

His shirt had come unfastened and Lindsay
longed to feel the male heat of his flesh against her
own. She reached out to touch him and then
withdrew, suddenly unsure and shy, but Lucas
took her hands and placed them on his skin,
swiftly unfastening the remaining buttons on his
shirt and drawing her hands against him, so that
she could feel the moist trembling of his body.

He rolled over on to his back, taking her with him, his tongue investigating the vulnerable hollow at the base of her throat. Her entire body seemed to be melting into his, and when his hands stroked down over her, cupping the rounded femininity of her bottom she moaned his name deep in her throat, completely possessed by the need for fulfilment that drove her on, timeless as life itself and just as enduring. Her fingers investigated the dark shadowing of his body hair following it downwards, her exploration forgotten when Lucas kissed her deeply, ravishing her senses, making her ache for the pleasure she knew instinctively he could give her.

She touched the waistband of his trousers, tentatively at first and then more surely as Lucas moaned his need to feel her touching him.

She had never undressed a man before and even with Lucas' help it seemed an aeon of time before his body was as naked as hers, gloriously and primitively masculine, making her pulses thud in an intensely feminine mixture of desire and fear, that had nothing really to do with her virginity and everything to do with the fact that he was male and powerful and she was female and held fast in thrall to that power . . .

'Lindsay.' He muttered her name rawly; impatiently almost taking her hands and drawing them against his body. 'Touch me,' he urged her huskily. 'Can't you see how much I need to feel you doing that? Do you enjoy tormenting me?' he demanded when she made no move to caress him.

Lindsay only shook her head, her voice thick with awe as she murmured wonderingly, 'You're beautiful . . .'

Dimly she was aware of Lucas laughing, the sound strained and faintly self-derisive, but she was too intent on taking in the masculine perfection of him to pay too much attention. She had always known that Lucas was entirely and completely male, but knowing and seeing that perfection were two different things. Wonderingly she touched the ridged muscles of his throat with her fingers and then her lips, amazed to feel his body clench beneath her caress. Her tongue touched a tiny bead of sweat on his chest, savouring the slight saltiness of it, her fingers ruffling the dark arrowing of hair.

'Lindsay for God's sake . . . what are you trying to do to me?'

The compressed savagery of his demand captured her attention. His face was white with strain, his eyes almost black, the pupils enlarged, the bones of his face starkly revealed by the tension of his expression.

'Do you *know* what you're doing to me?' he demanded, winding his fingers into her hair and tilting her head back so that he could look at her.

Tiny pulses of pleasure burned along her skin and she was instantly and acutely aware of an upsurge of feeling; of need, and yet perversely she still shook her head, as though in ignorance of what he meant.

'Show me.' The husky provocation of her own whispered words half shocked her. She had never thought to see herself play the seductress and certainly not with Lucas.

A glance into his dark, absorbed face, assured her that he felt no disgust or shock at her behaviour—quite the contrary, and her heart

leaped into her throat like a stranded fish as he
took her in his arms rolling her on to her back
trailing hungry kisses along her throat and down
to the valley between her breasts.

Lindsay held her breath remembering the
sensations the touch of his mouth against her
breasts had aroused, but he ignored their soft
fullness and instead moved down to her waist, his
teeth nibbling gently at her tender skin.

Quicksilver spurts of pleasure burned her skin,
and Lindsay moved wantonly in his arms, gasping
a heated protest as his lips moved slowly over her
stomach, his fingers drawing circles of delight
against her thigh.

An intense urgency thrilled through her, her
body arching wantonly against his, her breath
dying in her throat as he touched her intimately,
her flesh withdrawing shyly from the contact.

'No ... No, Lindsay let me touch you,' Lucas
demanded thickly, 'let me make love to you and
show you what it can be.'

The hoarse rasp of his voice, familiar and yet
unfamiliar soothed her fears, Lindsay let him
part her thighs and move between them, her
body welcoming the weight of his, her hips
lifting instinctively to move rhythmically against
his. He made a harsh sound of pleasure in his
throat, and Lindsay felt him tremble against her
as he muttered her name. She wanted the
maleness of him inside her more than she had
wanted anything before in her life. She ached
and yearned for it, to the extent that nothing ...
nothing else mattered. She felt him draw in a
sharp breath as her body invited his possession,
and then with a sound that was almost a groan

of despair he moved against and then swiftly inside her.

Her world was filled with alien sensations ... pain ... and something beyond it that urged her on; that encouraged the sure movement of Lucas' body within her own, a growing, aching sensation that gripped and possessed her making her cry out Lucas' name and cling desperately to him her only safe stronghold in the storm of passion that swept through her, leaving her drained and exalted; too exhausted to do more than lift her heavy lashes and look at him before exhaustion roared through her body and she fell deeply asleep.

CHAPTER NINE

WHEN Lindsay woke up she was alone. Late afternoon sunshine shone through her window. She moved under the protective cover of the bed clothes and winced as her muscles protested. A fine film of colour sprang up under her skin as she remembered what had occasioned those aches. Where was Lucas? As she struggled to sit up she saw a note propped up on her bedside table. It was from Lucas and said simply that he had been called out to the factory because of some crisis.

'When I come back we'll talk,' he had written at the end, and Lindsay felt suddenly chilled. No words of love or caring, but then what had she expected. Surely it must have been obvious even to her that Lucas was simply using her as a substitute for Gwen; as a means of ridding himself of his sexual frustration.

Unmercifully she lashed herself with bitter condemnation for her behaviour; for the fact that she must surely now have betrayed herself completely to Lucas, but nothing could make her entirely regret what had happened. They had been lovers, and Lucas had tenderly ... gloriously, initiated her into the mysteries of womanhood. But why? Not because he loved her as she loved him; that much she was sure of. It was pointless remembering the husky need in his voice, or the look in his eyes when he touched her ... when governed by desire as he had been, men were apt

to show all manner of emotions they were not
really feeling. Lucas hadn't set out deliberately to
deceive her . . . He had never said he loved her, for
instance. He had simply taken what she had so
wantonly offered. By the time she had been awake
for ten minutes, Lindsay had successfully convinced herself that Lucas had made love to her
only because she had explicitly invited him to do
so, and that all blame and responsibility for what
had happened was hers and hers alone. Lucas had
made love to her because, without saying so she
had shown him that she loved him; had mutely
begged him to do so, and no doubt during the
'talk' he intended to have with her; this would be
ruthlessly pointed out to her. Lucas didn't want
her around; she should have learned that years
ago.

Somehow she got herself dressed and downstairs,
and once there rather listlessly, she set about some
preparations for the evening meal. She had no idea
when Lucas would return, or even if he would
want to eat with her when he did, but at least
preparing some food for them both kept her hands
occupied, even if it left her mind free.

She and Lucas had been lovers. Even now she
found it hard to believe and yet she only had to
close her eyes to bring back a storm of memories
and sensations—sensations so strong that her
body still shook with the aftermath of them. Lucas
had been everything she had ever hoped for in a
lover. Tender, strong, exciting . . . compelling her
to give him a response that still had the power to
stun her. But he did not love her; not as she loved
him.

Tiredly placing the casserole in the oven,

Lindsay started to tidy up after herself. She had never felt less like eating . . . nor less able to face Lucas for the 'talk' his note mentioned. What was there for them to talk about? She already knew he did not love her; he surely must have guessed that she did love him. Lucas wasn't a fool—far from it. The fact that there had been no other men in her life must surely tell its own story. What would he do? Politely ask her to leave? Tell her the whole thing had been a mistake? Was she really strong enough to stay here and listen to him rationally explaining away what had happened between them until all that was left was the bitter after-taste of being forced to acknowledge that what for her had been the supreme moments of her life, for him had been merely a male reflex action and nothing more?

What alternative did she really have? She could leave; run away; refuse to talk with him. She could go now in fact, before he came back. They need never see one another again; that way at least her memories would remain intact. Recognising that she was on the verge of emotional hysteria, Lindsay tried to calm herself down. She was behaving like an adolescent not a woman. So Lucas had made love to her without loving her. It wasn't the end of the world. She had known he didn't love her before he even touched her. But Lucas had not known *she* loved *him*, she reminded herself and now that he did know; could hardly avoid knowing, he must surely be anxious to get her out of his life. If she had any pride she would go now before he was forced to spell it out for her. She would be saving them both embarrassment and awkwardness if she went.

She was just hesitating indecisively in the hallway when she heard the sound of Lucas' car. Now it was too late for her to run. He came in while she was still in the hall, looking tired and unbelievably filthy, his face, hands and shirt front black.

'There was a fire down at the warehouse,' he told her briefly before she could speak. 'Luckily no real damage was done and its under control now. I'm going up for a shower. Any chance of anything to eat?'

The casserole wouldn't be ready for quite some time, but she could make him an omelette Lindsay decided, nodding her head.

'Thanks.'

He didn't say anything else; made no reference to the 'talk' he wanted to have with her. In fact, there was no difference in his attitude towards her at all, if she discounted the disturbing way in which his glance had lingered first on her mouth and then on her body. You're imagining things she told herself as she walked into the kitchen. Why should Lucas look at you like a man dying of thirst looking on water? You're seeing what you want to see; distorting reality because you can't bear to face the truth.

Lucas was a long time coming back downstairs. The omelette mixture was ready to cook. She had brewed some fresh coffee, and buttered some fresh wholemeal bread, but there was no sign of the man she had made these preparations for. Feeling concerned Lindsay went upstairs rather hesitantly. Had Lucas changed his mind about wanting something to eat? He had looked tired enough to be close to exhaustion when he came in; he was such a strong, determined man that it was easy to forget how recently he had been ill. Fresh fear feathered along her nerve endings, and when her knock on his door evoked no response, Lindsay turned the handle and walked in, coming to an abrupt and unsteady halt.

Lucas was sprawled out on his bed, lying on his side, his skin still damp from his shower, the towel he had been using damp and crumpled beneath him. The faint beginnings of a beard darkened his jaw and in sleep his lashes fanned darkly against his skin with an odd vulnerability. Should she wake him, or should she let him sleep? Undecided she walked closer to the bed, her nerve endings jumping in quick alarm when, without warning his lashes swept up and he looked at her.

'Lindsay?'

It was too late to turn and run now, with his fingers curling round her wrist, tugging her towards him; her senses awash with the clean male scent of his body, and the irresistible attraction of his lean male frame. Beads of damp glistened against his skin. Impelled by some force she could neither understand nor deny Lindsay leaned forward, touching her tongue to the damp contour of his shoulder.

It was like setting alight a tinder-dry bonfire, the intensity of Lucas' response sending shivering waves of pleasure shuddering through her, encouraging her to lap eagerly at the moistness of his skin.

The pressure of his fingers gripping her was almost painful, the hoarse sounds of pleasure he muted against her throat triggering off further shock waves of desire that threatened to engulf them both.

Hazily Lindsay was aware of Lucas undressing her, cupping and caressing her breasts, stroking away the layers of civilisation and restraint as he stroked away her clothes, inciting her to arch and writhe in feminine provocation, touching him as he was touching her, melting ... aching ... engulfed by the intensity of her response to him and wanting more, much more than the silken glide of his hands over her skin.

The shrill sound of the telephone pierced through their golden cloud of pleasure. Lucas curled her against his body with one hand whilst the other lifted the receiver. As she looked into his face Lindsay saw it grow darker and harder as he listened to whoever was on the other end of the line, and then he said grimly, handing her the receiver, 'It's for you.'

Hesitantly Lindsay took the receiver from him, the colour leaving her face as she heard Jeremy's hectoring, slurred voice. 'With your lover are you? I suppose I should have expected that. Couldn't wait to jump into bed with him could you, you bitch ... but there's only one thing he wants from you Lindsay and that's your money ...'

She dropped the receiver as though it burned, Jeremy's drunken insults filling the tense silence of the room as the invective continued to pour out of him on a damning tide. Shivering with reaction and shock Lindsay got to her feet, gathering up her clothes. Lucas made no attempt to stop her as she fled towards the door. Nor did he follow her into the sanctuary of her own room.

She knew quite well that Jeremy had been drunk and that his accusations of Lucas wanting her for her father's wealth were completely unfounded.

But why hadn't he come after her? Why hadn't he taken her back in his arms and comforted her? Because he was already regretting that she had ever been there ... *She* had been the one to initiate their lovemaking ... It was true that concern and not lust had taken her to his room, but Lucas wasn't to know that. Waking up and finding her bending towards him like that he had interpreted her actions in a different way. He had thought she had come looking for him because she wanted to make love. She closed her eyes letting the hot bitter tears seep through them. Dear God, how he must despise her. What on earth was she to do.

She woke up half-way through the night cold and cramped to realise that she must have fallen asleep curled up where she was. It seemed like hours before she was able to get back to sleep again and when morning finally came she was heavy eyed and tense.

She found evidence that Lucas had been up before her in the kitchen where he had propped a note up against the coffee pot simply saying rather tersely that he had gone out to the factory and would be back later. This time there was no mention of any 'talk'. Had what happened last night made him wary of coming into *any* sort of contact with her?

One thing was sure, she could not stay here any longer.

She wasn't hungry and after making herself a cup of coffee she wandered listlessly into the drawing room. When she had woken up properly she would put her cases in her car and drive back to London. Sighing faintly she lay back in her arm chair closing her eyes. They were so sore and gritty. Well what did she expect after crying herself to sleep, Lindsay thought sardonically. The sound of the doorbell ringing jerked at her nerve endings. It was hardly likely to be Lucas, an inner voice scorned her; mocking her tension.

She got to her feet stiffly and walked toward the door. Callers were the last thing she felt capable of dealing with right now. She opened the door and stood blinking in the bright shaft of sunlight for several seconds shock pouring through her in an icy cold flood as she became aware of the identity of the woman standing there.

'My goodness someone didn't waste much time did they?' she drawled coolly.

'Gwen!'

Lucas' ex-wife was the last person Lindsay had expected to see.

'Aren't you going to invite me in?'

The faint American drawl in the other woman's voice was new, but the glossy, expensively packaged image she projected wasn't, and Lindsay could well remember how Gwnendolin had intimidated her as a teenager. Now she could just see the beginnings of a faint tracery of lines round her eyes; a faint hardening of her expression, but Gwen was still a very beautiful woman; and still a very predatory one, Lindsay suspected.

'I haven't got all day Lindsay,' she said sharply now. 'Frank is waiting for me in the village. I didn't think it was wise to bring him up here with me.'

'Lucas isn't here,' Lindsay told her dully, standing to one side so that she could walk into the hall.

'Naturally not.' The pencilled eyebrows rose.

'You surely didn't think I'd be here if I thought he was?' Bitterness compressed her mouth for a second.

'You're not ... You haven't come back to him then?' Lindsay asked dully.

'Come back to him.' Gwen laughed, a high sharp sound. 'My God that's rich. No I haven't. What I *have* come for is my jewellery. I didn't take it with me when I left. Unless you've any objections I'd like to go up to my room and get it.'

Her room? Lindsay frowned.

'Look why don't you wait until Lucas comes back,' she suggested weakly, 'Then you could see him ... talk to him ...'

Why was she doing this? Why was she laying up more pain for herself by trying to persuade Gwen to wait and see Lucas? Because she loved him so much that if Gwen was what he wanted; then Gwen was what she wanted him to have, she acknowledged forlornly.

'*See* him? *Talk* to him?' Gwen laughed harshly. 'To what purpose?' She shook her head. 'No, I've done all my seeing and talking to your precious Lucas.'

Lindsay turned to watch her mount the stairs. At the top she turned not towards Lucas' room but to one of the others. It was perhaps only natural that Lucas should choose to sleep in a room that did not remind him of his ex-wife, Lindsay reflected watching her, her heart aching with pain and love for him.

Gwen wasn't gone long. Within ten minutes she was coming back downstairs carrying several jewellery cases. 'Oh you needn't look like that,' she told Lindsay curtly. 'There's nothing here that came from Lucas.' She must have betrayed her shock in her face, Lindsay thought afterwards, because Gwen smiled mirthlessly, and said, 'Oh don't look down your nose at me, Miss. It's your precious Lucas whose at fault this time. No woman . . . no real woman that is, could live as he forced me to live . . . Like a nun . . .'

Pain tightened round Lindsay's throat like a clamp, but still she felt compelled to speak. 'It's only natural that Lucas wouldn't want his wife to have lovers,' she felt bound to say.

Inwardly she thought it was typical of Gwen and her selfishness to cause Lucas further pain by coming back—not to see him, but to collect the jewellery bestowed upon her by other men.

'Is it? Why?' Gwen demanded tightly. 'So that I should be as celibate as he is himself . . . as sexless as he is? You think I'm lying,' she added mirthlessly, when Lindsay stared at her in a disbelieving silence. 'Well what else would you call a man who doesn't make love to his wife?'

'You don't believe me? Ask Tom Henry . . . He knows . . . He was the one who found us a solicitor discreet enough to put through the annulment of our marriage quietly. Don't think I don't know why he couldn't make love to me either,' she hissed at Lindsay, the mask of sophistication brutally stripped from her face. 'It was because of *you*. *You* ruined my marriage. You with your simpering stupid adolescent ways . . . You got under his skin, making him want you. Oh he thought I didn't know why he'd married me . . . that he was using me to hide behind, but I knew all right. What I didn't bargain for was a man so besotted by a teenager that he couldn't bear to

touch me.' Anger and frustration glinted for a
second in her eyes and Lindsay realised the older
woman was not seeing her, but looking back into
the past. Her revelations were both shocking and
unbelievable. Lucas? Sexless ... Lucas ...?

'Don't get your hopes up though,' Gwen told
her savagely. 'He'll never make love to you, never
marry you. His duty to your father will see to
that ... It's laughable really, the great Lucas
Armitage an impotent hulk of a man incapable of
making love to a woman ... a real woman that is
not some stupid, mooning teenager.'

That's not true! Lindsay wanted to shout the
words at her, but they stuck in her throat.

'You can tell him why I came,' Gwen threw
casually over her shoulder at Lindsay as she
walked through the open front door, 'and what I
told you. Don't hope too hard that he'll deny it,
will you? You know, it almost makes up for
everything. Knowing how much he wants you and
that he can't have you.'

It couldn't possibly be true ... None of it could
be true. Lindsay sat down heavily on the stairs,
her numb brain trying to come to terms with all
that Gwen had said. By implication she had told
her that Lucas had never loved his wife; could not
possibly be mourning her as she, Lindsay had
thought ... That quite to the contrary ... Lucas
loved *her*! But that was impossible. He had never
... He *had* made love to her an inner voice
reminded her ... he had touched and kissed her
like a starving man faced with food ... He had ...
Stop it ... stop it, she warned herself, not wanting
to get too carried away on the euphoria of the
moment. Gwen could easily have been lying to her,

wanting to hurt her by holding out false hope to
her. Gwen had always known how she felt about
Lucas. But surely Gwen would not have mentioned
Tom if she had been lying. One way to discover
the truth was simply to ask Lucas, she reminded
herself, but she quailed from taking such a step.
Even if it was true, he would probably deny it,
especially if, as Gwen had claimed he felt honour
bound to conceal his feelings for her because he
knew that her father ... Sighing faintly Lindsay
got to her feet. Was there any way she could find
out the truth? Yes, Tom would know ... but
would he tell her? There was only one way to find
out.

Filled with a sudden surge of energy that
banished the exhaustion and misery from her
body, she got into her car and drove into Malden.

Tom was with a client when she went into his
office, but Mary was able to tell her that he should
be free within half an hour, and Lindsay elected to
wait. A storm of butterflies seemed to have been
released into her nervous system. She wasn't going
to even let herself hope; it all seemed far too
improbable ... Like something out of a romantic
novel, with the hero nobly giving up the girl he
loved for some quixotic notion of honour. Fear
coiled along her spine. What if it *was* true? How
was she going to persuade Lucas. . .? One step at a
time she cautioned herself. It was pointless trying
to deal with problems before she encountered
them. Tom might tell her that Gwen had been
telling her a pack of lies, and then ...

Only when she contemplated it did she realise
how much hope she had pinned on Gwen telling
the truth. It frightened her to realise how much her

very ability to live and function normally was dependent on knowing she had Lucas' love. Without it the world was an intolerably cold and inhospitable place. Unknowingly her face took on a sombre, forlorn expression, and it was this that first caught Tom Henry's attention when he came out of his office with his departing client.

'Lindsay, my dear,' he greeted her, hiding his concern. 'Two visits in one week ... I am indeed honoured.'

Lindsay could hardly bear to waste time in preliminaries and polite exchanges, but she forced herself to do so, letting Tom usher her into his office and sit her down opposite himself.

'Well now . . .'

'Tom ... it's about Lucas and Gwen's divorce.' She stumbled into hasty speech, the words tumbling over one another in her anxiety and despair.

Tom Henry listened carefully to what she was saying, his expression betraying nothing, other than a certain sad compassion, as she stumbled through her story.

'Is it true?' she asked quietly at last. 'Was their marriage annulled because. . .?'

'Because they were never truly man and wife?' Tom supplemented for her. 'Yes, Lindsay it is. I shouldn't really be discussing any of this with you, you realise that don't you?' he went on to say, 'but since you are so closely involved ...' He sighed, and spoke into his intercom. 'Mary could we have some coffee in here please ... Try to relax,' he told Lindsay. 'This could take quite some time. Perhaps I'd better begin at the beginning.'

He paused when Mary brought in their coffee,

whilst Lindsay was mentally seething with impatience and agitation. When Mary had closed the door behind her Tom leaned forward, elbows on his desk, finger-tips together, a frown creasing his forehead. Was he doing the right thing? Did he have the right to talk to Lindsay about what, after all, was an intensely private thing? When Lucas had talked to him at the time he had offered the opinion that Lucas should do what *he* wanted . . . not what he thought Lindsay's father had wanted. *Then* he had chosen to ignore him.

He sighed faintly again.

'Lucas' marriage was annulled—yes. When Gwen told him that she wanted to marry someone else, he approached me for legal advice. As I told you I recommended a friend of mine to him who specialises in family law. There was no problem with the annulment—that was all straightforward, and Lucas was extremely generous in what he settled on Gwen—your father left him in sole charge of the business and it has progressed extremely profitably under his Chairmanship—Lucas is a comfortably wealthy young man.

'However, Gwen was extremely bitter about their marriage. She even threatened to make the reasons for their break-up public locally. Fortunately she changed her mind.'

'She said that Lucas married her because of me, because he . . .'

'Certainly you were one of his considerations when he married,' Tom interrupted hastily. 'As you already know there was a considerable amount of gossip at the time of your father's death. You were barely seventeen—Lucas older, but far from old enough to be considered in the light of a guardian. There was no blood tie between you, and as Lucas has since admitted to me, he knew then that he ... desired you. He married Gwen to safeguard you, Lindsay. As much from himself as from any gossip I suspect.'

'From himself?'

Tom grimaced faintly. 'Yes, Lindsay. Surely you realise that he loved you ... And still does I suspect. Only his respect and the duty he felt he owed your father stopped him from marrying you himself. I know that much because he told me so. I did tell him at the time that I felt he was carrying loyalty to your father too far ... but he wouldn't listen ...'

'I knew there was gossip of course,' Lindsay murmured, barely registering the fact that Tom was still talking. She was back in the past in those early months after her father's death when Lucas had changed from the most approachable and caring person in her life to a distant stranger. 'I even thought that Gwen was deliberately manufacturing half of it. She made it quite plain that she wanted Lucas.'

'Yes I know. As does Lucas. He never made any pretence of loving Gwen. She knew what the position was when she married him, Lucas admitted to me that he had intended the marriage to be a completely viable one. Gwen was and still is an extremely attractive woman, but ...' He shrugged and looked embarrassed. Poor Tom, Lindsay thought sympathetically. He was obviously finding the whole discussion difficult, and no wonder. She was still having trouble coming to terms with it.

'You said that Lucas still loves me,' she managed to whisper at last.

'Well yes, or at least so I suspect.'

'Why didn't you tell me any of this the last time I was here. You guessed how I feel about him.'

'My dear it was hardly my place,' he cautioned her gently. 'If Lucas has not chosen to tell you himself then . . .'

'Then he still prefers to remain loyal to my father than to admit his love for me, is that what you're trying to say?'

'You must try to understand Lindsay. Lucas feels he owes your father everything. You know yourself how adamant your father was about your marriage, but I will tell you this. There was no one your father liked and respected as much as he did Lucas.'

'All this time I thought he loved Gwen . . . that he was missing her and that, that . . .' Lindsay was lost in her own thoughts, a hectic flush colouring her skin as she remembered how Lucas had touched and caressed her. All the time he had loved *her* and not Gwen, at least if Tom was to be believed. But what good did his loving her do. when he refused to admit it to her . . . when he refused to treat her as anything other than an annoying responsibility. Lucas was a very stubborn man and it would take greater strength and willpower than she possessed to move him from a course, once he was set upon it.

But he *had* made love to her, a traitorous voice of hope reminded her. He had wanted her . . . loved her to such an extent that his need had overruled what he considered to be his duty. Surely that must mean something . . .

Something perhaps, but what? Perhaps if she

could just get him to admit how he felt about her
... that he did love her. With an effort Lindsay
tried to concentrate on what Tom was saying.

'Do you really think he loves me, Tom?' she
asked at length.

Sensing the need behind the question he smiled at
her. 'Yes I do Lindsay, but equally as strong as his
love for you are his feelings for your father. He's a
man torn between two opposing desires. For years
he's taken one course ... whether you'll be able to
distract him from it, I wouldn't like to say.'

'My father loved and respected Lucas as well,'
Lindsay said slowly, 'and I can't honestly and
truly believe in my heart of heart's that if he knew
how we felt about one another that he would
seriously want to keep us apart; to make us both
suffer, do you?'

'No,' Tom told her decisively. 'Had your father
lived; had he realised how you both felt I feel sure
he would have changed his mind, and welcomed
Lucas into the family as his son-in-law. In fact I'm
convinced of it.'

Lindsay smiled wanly at him. '*You* may be, but I
suspect it will take a great deal to convince Lucas
of it.'

She kissed Tom warmly before leaving, a new
strength slowly growing inside her as she headed
for her car. She loved Lucas and he loved her; and
surely that love was worth fighting for? As she
headed for home she made her plans. It would take
guts and nerves of steel, but ... nothing ventured
... Compressing her fears, she told herself that
nothing would be gained by encouraging doubts.
She must think positive. She must first convince
herself that she had the power to convince Lucas.

CHAPTER TEN

MORE than once as the long hours of the afternoon dragged by and she waited for Lucas to come home, Lindsay had doubts. It seemed impossible to believe that he loved her; that he had in fact loved her for years and kept that love hidden from her, but it was true, she reassured herself fiercely. It was true.

Unable to settle, she paced the rooms of the empty house, arguing with herself, trying to see the situation from Lucas' point of view as well as her own. Her father had loved them both. Would he honestly have wanted them to be unhappy and apart? She shook her head tiredly. It didn't matter how much she could reassure herself if she couldn't convince Lucas. She wandered into the kitchen remembering that last night's uneaten casserole was in the fridge. It seemed a singularly unglamorous meal to serve to a man whom she was about to tell she loved.

More to keep herself occupied than anything else she examined the contents of the freezer and larder; mentally planning out a more enticing menu from their contents.

Six o'clock came and went and Lucas still had not returned. Lindsay began to panic that he did not intend to do so. Perhaps he was staying away in the hope that she would leave. Her face grew hot as she remembered how she had touched him; betraying her feelings for him. But he had touched

her too, she reminded herself stalwartly ... the
need and longing; the love had not all been on her
side.

It was just gone seven when she eventually heard
the familiar sound of Lucas' car tyres on the gravel
drive.

He came in looking drained; exhausted almost.

'You're late.'

How banal and domesticated she sounded
Lindsay thought wryly, but how else could she
greet him? Hi Lucas ... by the way I know that
you love me? Hardly.

'I had a meeting with our insurers and it
dragged on longer than planned. They thought
initially there might have been some contributory
negligence on the part of the company that caused
the fire, but in the end they backed down. It was a
long fight though.'

'I thought the purpose of carrying insurance was
for protection, not in order to fight,' Lindsay
commented wryly.

'Everything in life is a fight, Lindsay,' Lucas
retorted. 'Haven't you learned that yet?'

Perhaps he was right. If so, she was certainly
going to fight for the right to love him, she decided
firmly. She wasn't going to stand tamely aside
because his notions of what he owed her father
precluded him from loving her.

She forced herself to adopt self-control and
withhold all that she was aching to say to him
until after they had eaten dinner. He raised his
eyebrows a little when he saw how she had done
the table, using the best crystal and silver, but he
stopped short of making any comment.

She managed to concoct a fresh fruit starter

with what she had found in the fridge, and as she watched him eat she was pleased to see the tiredness ebbing out of his face. He had showered and shaved while she was putting the final touches to their meal, and Lindsay was unbearably aware of him despite the length of the table between them.

He was dressed casually in jeans and a thin silk shirt open at the neck and her heart started to pound in heavy uneven thuds as she looked at him.

She waited until after dinner, when they were sitting in the drawing room drinking coffee, to launch her attack, saying casually, 'Oh by the way I had a visitor today.'

'Yes?'

'Gwen,' she informed him as nonchalantly as she could, bending over to fill his coffee cup so that he could not see her face, but she could his. A tiny muscle flickered momentarily in his jaw, but other than that he betrayed no response.

'She came to collect her jewellery,' Lindsay informed him. 'She didn't stay very long.'

She could sense his tension and thought of abandoning her self-imposed task. She couldn't bear to hurt him, and yet so much was at stake.

'I was surprised how little she's changed,' Lindsay added. 'Hardly at all. She's as sophisticated and lovely as ever.'

Lucas made a non-committal sound and picked up his coffee.

'I'm sorry,' she apologised insincerely, 'I know you still love her . . . I shouldn't be talking about her to you.'

Lucas replaced his coffee cup and looked at her.

His eyes were dark grey and unfathomable, angry chips of steel that warned her that she was treading on very treacherous ground.

'All right Lindsay,' he said tightly. 'I can't pretend to know what game you're playing. Just what are you trying to say.'

His direct attack flustered her. 'No game ... why should I....?'

'That's what I keep asking myself,' he agreed dryly, 'and I still haven't come up with a satisfactory answer, so suppose you answer the question for me.'

'Gwen told me about your marriage being annulled,' she told him baldly, dropping her glance from his face to his chest, as she flinched from the cold unmoving scrutiny of his eyes. 'She told me that you ... she ... that you never slept together,' she floundered on. Damn him why wasn't he helping her? Why was he deliberately making it harder for her.

'Did she? Then she lied,' he told her impassively, 'As I recall it sleeping together was one of the few things we did do. All right Lindsay,' he said curtly, 'So you know that our marriage was annulled ... so what's the big deal?'

'I also know *why* it was annulled,' Lindsay told him bravely taking a deep breath and praying that her courage would hold out. He was deliberately using his experience and male power to try and beat her down ... to make *her* back down but she wasn't going to do so.

'So ... Lucas shrugged. 'The very fact that it was annulled speaks for itself. The marriage was never consummated.'

'No ... not that ... I didn't mean ... what I

meant was I know . . . I know *why* it wasn't
consummated,' Lindsay interrupted desperately.
Dear God, this wasn't turning out at all as she
planned. By this stage Lucas should have been the
one on the run, admitting to her that he had loved
her. Instead . . .

'Oh?' She had all his attention now, every
narrow eyed, nerve racking ounce of it. Licking
dry lips anxiously Lindsay fought not to shy away
from the intensity of his gaze.

'Gwen told me your marriage was annulled
because . . . because you . . . because she considers
that you were impotent,' she managed at last. 'I
know that isn't true . . . So I went to see Tom and
he . . . that is . . . He told me he thought you love
me,' she said baldly at last.

The silence that followed her statement was
appalling.

'I see.' Lucas said the words softly, in a tone
infused with a taunting mockery that made
Lindsay's blood freeze. 'My, my what a romantic
little mind you're hiding away under that modern
exterior. Do tell me how you managed to deduce
from the brief facts available to you, this
marvellous theory that I'm in love with you? That
was what you said wasn't it?' he asked with cool
irony. 'Fantastic . . . Ever thought of taking up
fiction writing for a living?' His glance lashed her
over-sensitive nerves. She could have cried out
with pain and anguish, but pride would not let her.
She had handled it all wrong and now Lucas was
punishing her. Punishing her in such a way that
would ensure that she never, ever raised the
subject again.

'There's no need for all the play-acting Lucas,'

she managed to interrupt. 'If I'm wrong then all you have to do is tell me quite simply that you don't love me.'

'I thought that was exactly what I was doing,' he returned with acid irony.

She wanted to turn and run then, to bury herself away where no one could find her and witness her agony. How could she ever have been deranged enough to persuade herself that he could actually care. Anger ... resentment ... these she had been prepared for but not this cool mocking sarcasm, that burned agonising pain into her heart and soul.

'Do enlighten me further,' he continued in that same icily derisive tone, refusing to end her ordeal. 'When was I supposed to have er ... conceived this grand passion for you?'

'When I was seventeen.' Lindsay felt her skin burning beneath his raised eyebrows and surprised look.

'Really?' Tom told you that did he?'

'He said he thought you loved me years ago,' Lindsay told him tiredly, too beaten to care any more what she betrayed to him. 'He felt that you'd married Gwen in part to protect me from gossip ...'

'That much at least has some slight spark of truth in it,' he agreed, 'At the time it seemed a reasonable course to take. Gwen had made it plain that she coveted the role of my wife. She was, and is, as you say, a very beautiful woman ... It was time I was married ...'

'You let me think you *loved* her ... That you still loved her ...'

He shrugged aside her comment and Lindsay said despairingly, 'Why can't you be honest with

me . . . Why did you make love to me if you don't
care for me . . .'

'Why did you let me?'

It was curtly spoken and Lindsay held her
breath, wanting to retain this last final barrier of
pride, but knowing that if relinquishing it was
what it took to win Lucas' love, then relinquish it
she must.

'Because I love you,' she told him quietly. 'I
realised the truth when you were ill,' she continued
dispiritedly. 'When I look back I can see now that
I always loved you, but I wouldn't face up to the
truth because . . .'

'Because it didn't fit in with what you'd been
brought up to expect. Marriage to a man who
fitted all your father's specifications. Unlike me.'

'But daddy loved you . . . He respected and
admired you,' Lindsay burst out. 'You *know* he
did.'

'He also appointed me as one of your Trustees
to make sure that his wishes in respect to your
marriage were carried out,' Lucas reminded her
hardily. 'Even if I *did* love you would you honestly
expect me to break the trust he placed in me?'

'Yes,' Lindsay whispered in agonised pain. 'Yes,
Lucas, if you loved me the way I love you then
you would do so, because to live without me
would be impossible.' She turned away from him
unable to bear to look at him any longer. What a
fool she had been. He *didn't* love her and never
had. Tom had been completely wrong about that.

'I'd better leave,' she said quietly, standing up.
'There's no point in my staying on here now.'

'None at all,' Lucas agreed curtly. A small
muscle beat sporadically in his jaw, and his eyes

were veiled from her so that she couldn't read his expression. She was a fool to go on hoping that by some miracle he would change his mind and tell her that he loved her. A complete and utter fool.

It didn't take her long to go upstairs and bring down her cases. She had thrown her clothes haphazardly into them, not really caring what she packed and what she left. Clothes could always be replaced.

She stowed them in the boot of her car and started the engine. Dusk was falling. and she refused to look in the direction of the drawing room window to see if Lucas was watching her. He wasn't. He was striding towards the car, and even now, ridiculously, hope flared, only to die as she saw his set, tense expression.

'You may think you love me now, Lindsay,' he said tersely, 'but one day you'll thank me for this . . .'

'For what?' she demanded tersely, 'Breaking my heart and my pride, throwing my love back in my face . . . How will I thank you Lucas. By making things easy for you by marrying someone my father would have approved of? If you really feel like that why didn't you encourage me to marry Jeremy. He was everything Daddy wanted for me.'

'He didn't love you.' He said it slowly, as though the words were being dragged out of him under torture.

His pseudo-concern made Lindsay shake with hysterical laughter. It pealed out wildly into the thick silence of the evening. Her fingers curled round the steering wheel, her foot jabbing hard on the accelerator as she turned her car round. Before she drove away she called out bitterly, 'You've got what you wanted Lucas. I'm leaving, and you're safe . . . safe from me . . . safe from my love.'

Once she was clear of the village she had to pull in and get her body back under control. She was shaking violently with reaction and pain. He didn't love her . . . how could he?

Tom was an astute man, another inner voice contradicted her. He would not have told her he thought Lucas loved her if he had been in any doubt at all. But how *could* he love her and send her away like that? Perhaps because he was desperate. Desperate men have been known to do almost superhuman things. Telling herself that she was weak and stupid Lindsay re-started her car and drove on.

She was half-way back to London before she admitted she wasn't going to complete the journey. She *had* to go back and see Lucas. She *had* to hear from his own lips the words, 'I do not love you'. She *had* to.

Telling herself she was all kinds of fool made no difference. She had already taken the next turn off the motorway and was heading back.

When she reached it the house was all in darkness. For a moment she thought Lucas must be out, but then she saw his car. She parked her own next to it, making no attempt to muffle the sound of her arrival. The front door was unlocked and she walked nervously into the dark hall snapping on the lights. A quick tour of the downstairs rooms proved that Lucas wasn't in any of them. In the study she found an empty tumbler and she sniffed it curiously. Whisky. Lucas rarely drank. But where was he?

She went upstairs slowly, already regretting her

own impetuosity but too stubborn to back down and leave.

A thin band of light showed under Lucas' bedroom door. As his room faced the rear of the house, she hadn't seen the light when she drove up. She knocked and held her breath. There was no response. Pushing open the door, Lindsay halted on the threshhold. Lucas was lying across the bed, his shirt unfastened, his hair ruffled and untidy.

A half empty bottle of whisky stood on the bedside table, an empty glass on the floor at his feet. He had made no attempt to get undressed other than to unfasten his shirt and kick off his shoes, and as she walked over to him Lindsay could smell the strong odour of the spirit he had drunk. Lucas drunk? It seemed impossible, and yet the heavy torpor of his sleep bore out her suspicions as did the half empty bottle beside him. She snapped off the overhead light and switched on the softer bedside lamp, a wave of mingled tenderness and pain washing over her. Of their own volition her fingers reached out and smoothed the tousled hair back off his forehead. Lucas moved restlessly beneath her touch, frowning heavily.

'Lucas . . .' She called his name softly, but there was no response other than another frown. Quickly Lindsay removed his clothes, and then shed her own, without giving herself time to mull over the morality of her actions.

Covering them both with his duvet she reached out and touched him lightly, stroking her fingers over his skin, murmuring his name over and over again.

In his sleep his body relaxed against her. He muttered something under his breath and she held her own, watching his lashes flicker. What would she say when he woke up?

'Lindsay?' He stared at her in the dim light, his voice slurred and hesitant.

'Yes, it's me Lucas.' She was still touching him and she pressed herself up against him now, placing her lips to his shoulder. She felt the frisson of response that ran through him and knew a heady satisfaction. Sexually at least he was responsive to her; he couldn't deny *that*.

'You came back.' His voice was stronger now. 'Why?'

'Because I love you,' she said quietly, 'and I won't believe you don't love me until you hold me like this and tell me so . . . Do it Lucas,' she invited huskily, moving her body against his. 'Tell me you don't want me . . . That you don't love me. I love you Lucas,' she continued before he could speak, 'and if my father had lived he'd have realised that no one else could make me happy. I can't *make* you love me in return, I know that, but maybe I'm already carrying your child . . . a part of you that no one can take away from me. I hope so. What would my father think of that Lucas? Do you think he'd approve of you leaving me to bear your child alone?'

'Damn you Lindsay, you can't do this to me.' The words were thick and unsteady, his body responding mindlessly to the feminine enticement of her own. His fingers locked round her upper arms—to thrust her away Lindsay was sure, but instead they held her against him, her breasts pressed against his chest, stimulated by the erotic contact with his flesh. She kissed his shoulder and then his neck, letting her tongue trace a delicate line upwards. She could feel him shuddering against her and knew a tiny thrill of pleasure that she was able to arouse him.

'Lindsay, for God's sake, what are you trying to do to me?' His mouth covered hers, his kiss that of a man starved for the feel of the woman he loves in his arms. Lindsay responded to him mindlessly, saying nothing, letting their bodies communicate for them. He made love to her with passion and need, overwhelming her with a hunger so intense that she trembled beneath it. He still hadn't answered her question an hour later when he fell asleep in her arms. Sighing faintly, Lindsay curled up against him. Tonight he had made love to her . . . who knew perhaps tomorrow he might tell her with words as well as actions that Tom had been right and that he did care. Too exhausted to think any more she fell asleep.

It was Lucas' voice in her ear that woke her the next morning.

'So I didn't dream it,' he said slowly. 'Did I dream you saying you loved me, and that you hoped you'd conceive my child?'

Lindsay couldn't see his face, so she shook her head and said huskily, 'No you didn't dream it, any more than I dreamed you saying last night that you didn't love me and that you couldn't marry me because my father would not have approved,' she finished bravely.

Lucas curled his fingers round her jaw and tilted her head up so that he could look into her eyes. He looked extremely masculine and slightly raffish with a night's beard darkening his jaw, Lindsay thought dreamily.

'Part of that at least was the truth,' he said wryly, 'and after last night I'm sure I don't need to tell you which part.'

'Well I know you believe my father would not have approved of us marrying,' Lindsay ventured, 'but we don't need his approval Lucas, and besides, I'm nearly sure, and Tom agrees with me, that if he'd lived nothing would have pleased him more than for us to marry. You were the son he never had.'

'Cast in his own image,' Lucas admitted, 'but not the man he wanted for his daughter . . . no matter how much than man might want her.'

Lindsay's heart leapt at this tacit admission that he did care, but she didn't take him up on it, teasing him instead. 'Which do you think my father would have preferred Lucas—that you married his daughter or that you seduced her.'

'*I* seduce *you*?' But he was smiling at last. 'When you were seventeen I sent you away, cut myself off from you because I thought it was the right thing to do . . . but I've never stopped wishing things could have been different . . . I'm not the man your father would have wanted for you Lindsay.'

'You're the man *I* want,' she told him gently, 'and besides you owe me something . . . I haven't forgotten that it's partially your fault that I lost Jeremy. You *could* have told him that we weren't lovers, but you didn't did you?'

'If he really thought so little of you he deserved to lose you,' Lucas said contemptuously. 'Dear God couldn't he *see* what you were . . . how innocent . . .'

'Why should he,' Lindsay teased. 'You didn't. You thought I'd had umpteen lovers . . .'

'Umm, and tormented myself with jealousy over every one of them. Every time you mentioned a man's name I imagined you going to bed with him . . . I dreaded you coming down here and telling me you were getting married . . .'

'You did a remarkable job of keeping your feelings hidden,' Lindsay told him. 'I thought you loved Gwen. I thought you were just using me as a substitute for her.'

'The idea was correct, you just got the cast the wrong way round.' He grimaced slightly. 'Have you any idea what it was like not being able to make love to my wife because I was obsessed with a seventeen-year-old teenager—and one who was my stepsister. Your father wouldn't have wanted this for you, Lindsay,' he told her wryly.

'I want it for myself.' She sounded fiercely stubborn. 'Do you really want to see me married to someone like Jeremy. Forced to make the same mistakes in my marriage that you made in yours. Only women aren't men Lucas,' she reminded him cruelly. 'Their bodies don't protect them from the consequences of their actions. Unlike yours my marriage would have to be consummated.'

She winced when she saw his expression, hating herself for causing him such pain. How had she ever thought him uncaring or hard?

'God, Lindsay, you don't know what it does to me to think of you with someone else . . . anyone else.'

'Then don't think of it,' she said softly, 'whether you want me or not Lucas, I won't marry anyone else. I can't. Neither can I make you love me enough to put aside what you consider to be your loyalty to my father.'

'No, you can't make me do that,' he agreed, touching her face, tracing its outlines with tender fingers. 'I can fight myself, Lindsay, but I can't fight you. I can't look into your eyes and see them looking at me with love and need, and turn you away. You're all I've ever wanted from life, Lindsay. Right from the first time I looked at you, my funny little stepsister, and saw I was looking at a woman and not a child, and if I'm condemned to eternal hell for it, I still have to have you. I want you with me for the rest of my life, as my wife . . . the mother of my children . . . as my woman, the other half of me . . . and if that brands me as a traitor to your father, then so be it.' He bent his head and kissed her slowly, as though placing a seal upon his words. For a moment neither of them spoke and then Lindsay reached up to embrace him, to welcome him to the realm of their love.

A week later they were married by special licence. Tom Henry was there, and after the small informal wedding breakfast, he asked if he could see them both for a few minutes.

The reception had been held at the house, and slightly mystified Lucas and Lindsay followed him into the study. He held an envelope in his hands which he gave to them both. 'A wedding present from your father,' he told Lindsay quietly.

At first she thought it was the Trust Deed, transferring her father's wealth into her own name, but Tom still hadn't finished speaking.

'Three days before your parents' accident, your father called in to see me and gave me this letter,' he told Lindsay. 'I do know what it contains, but I promised him I would never speak of it—to either of you, and although just lately that's been rather hard, I stuck by that promise. You see Lindsay,' he continued, forestalling her questions, 'Whether your father had some indication of what was to happen or not I shouldn't like to say. All I will say is that he came to see me and told me that he'd been having second thoughts about the wisdom of revenging himself against your mother's people by pushing you into marriage with one of them. In fact it wasn't just second thoughts he'd had, but a complete change of heart. I don't know whether he guessed how you felt about Lindsay or not, Lucas, but he'd become convinced that you were the ideal man to take charge, not only of his business empire, but his daughter as well. In short he *wanted* the pair of you to marry, but he was wary of pushing you towards each other, because he felt so guilty about what he'd already tried to do. He made me promise to say nothing to either of you about his hopes. He wanted it to happen naturally, he told me. He wanted you to marry for love or not at all. What neither of us had bargained for was that the pair of you should stick so stubbornly to his original wishes. Many many times I've longed to be able to tell you the truth, but I gave him my word.' He sighed faintly. 'It isn't always easy playing *deus ex machine.*'

Lindsay smiled through her tears, ripping open the envelope and taking out her father's letter. It put down in his own words exactly what Tom had said.

Silently she handed it over to Lucas for him to read, and then both of them were silent. Tom let himself out of the study leaving them together.

'When I think of how close I came to refusing

your love,' Lucas shuddered deeply like a man emerging from an unpleasant dream.

'I can hardly believe it,' Lindsay admitted. 'That Daddy should have had such a complete change of heart . . .'

Lucas was nuzzling her ear, sending trickles of pleasure darting down her spine. 'I suppose this means now that we'll have to call our first son after him,' he mock grumbled.

'What son's that?' Lindsay asked dreamily, leaning against him, secure in the circle of his arms.

'The one you threatened me with in order to get me to marry you, hussy,' Lucas reminded her.

'Ah, yes, that one,' Lindsay agreed with a secret smile. 'Do you know Lucas,' she added thoughtfully, 'I'm still not sure whether or not . . .' She paused delicately and looked at him with hopeful encouragement . . .

'Later,' Lucas told her mock warningly. 'Remember we've still got a house full of wedding guests.'

'Oh I'm sure they wouldn't miss us,' she claimed provocatively. 'They're having far too much fun gossiping about how astonishing it is that we've got married . . . and so quickly.'

They both laughed and then Lucas bent his head and said softly to her. 'They might not miss you but I certainly would. So much so that I never intend to let you get more than an arm's length away from me.'

Beneath his lazy teasing, Lindsay could sense the controlled force of his love for her but she still couldn't resist asking hesitantly, 'Lucas, if I hadn't come back that night, if I . . .'

He placed his fingers against her lips to silence her. 'That half bottle of whisky I drank was by way of saying farewell to my self control and honour,' he told her wryly. 'I had already decided that first thing in the morning I was coming after you. I would have dragged you back with me if I'd needed to Lindsay. It didn't take more than ten minutes in the house without you for me to admit that my love for you was too strong for me to resist ... that despite what your father had wanted, I loved you ... and I was going to come after you and tell you exactly that. I was also going to get down on my knees if necessary to beg you to give me another chance.'

'You were!' Lindsay sighed theatrically. 'Damn, and I went and spoiled it all.'

A six-year-old guest looking for the cloakroom opened the study door, and then quickly shut it again, returning to the drawing room to announce rather breathlessly that she had just found the bride and groom kissing in the study. Her father tweaking one stubby blonde plait grinned over her head at her mother and said smilingly, 'Then let's just leave them to it shall we poppet. After all, that's what weddings are all about.'

Coming Next Month

Available in April wherever paperback books are sold, or through Harlequin Reader Service:

In the U.S.
P.O. Box 1397
Buffalo, N.Y.
14240-1397

In Canada
P.O. Box 2800, Postal Sation A
5170 Yonge Street
Willowdale, Ontario M2N 6J3

You're invited to accept 4 books and a surprise gift Free!

Acceptance Card

Mail to: **Harlequin Reader Service®**

In the U.S.	In Canada
901 Fuhrmann Blvd.	P.O. Box 2800, Postal Station A
P.O. Box 1394	5170 Yonge Street
Buffalo, N.Y. 14240-1394	Willowdale, Ontario M2N 6J3

YES! Please send me 4 free Harlequin Presents® novels and my free surprise gift. Then send me 8 brand new novels every month as they come off the presses. Bill me at the low price of $1.75 each ($1.95 in Canada)— an 11% saving off the retail price. There are no shipping, handling or other hidden costs. There is no minimum number of books I must purchase. I can always return a shipment and cancel at any time. Even if I never buy another book from Harlequin, the 4 free novels and the surprise gift are mine to keep forever.   108 BPP-BPGE

Name _____ (PLEASE PRINT)

Address _____ Apt. No. _____

City _____ State/Prov. _____ Zip/Postal Code _____

This offer is limited to one order per household and not valid to present subscribers. Price is subject to change.   ACP-SUB-1R